TANGLED WEB #1
TWISTED

TWISTED

Book #1 of the TANGLED WEB trilogy

Aleatha Romig

New York Times, Wall Street Journal, and USA Today
bestselling author of the Consequences, Infidelity, and Web of
Sin series

D1279153

COPYRIGHT AND LICENSE INFORMATION

TWISTED

2019 Edition License

TWISTED

BLURB

The underworld of Chicago is far from forgiving. It's a world where knowledge means power, power money, and money everything.

While I paid the ultimate price to have it all, it wasn't my decision to give my life.

That doesn't mean I ceased to exist, only to live.

Going where the job takes me and living in the shadows, with deadly accuracy I utilize the skills inherent to me, not knowing from where they came, not recalling what I'd lost.

And then I saw her.
Laurel Carlson.

I shouldn't want her, desire her, or need her, yet with each sighting I know she is exactly what I have to have. Laurel has the ability to do what I thought was impossible. She sees what others don't.

My gut tells me that it's a deadly mistake to change my plans and open my world to her. My mind says she'll be repulsed by my twisted existence.

None of that matters because my body won't take no for an answer.

I've made dangerous mistakes before.
This time, will the price be too high?

From New York Times bestselling author Aleatha Romig comes a brand-new dark romance set in the same dangerous underworld as *SECRETS*. You do not need to read the *Web of Sin* trilogy to get caught in this new and intriguing saga, *Tangled Web*.

TWISTED is book one of the *TANGLED WEB* trilogy which will continue in *OBSESSED* and conclude in *BOUND*.

Have you been Aleatha'd?

TANGLED WEB #1

TWISTED

TWISTED

Book #1 of the TANGLED WEB trilogy

Aleatha Romig

New York Times, Wall Street Journal, and USA Today
bestselling author of the Consequences, Infidelity, and Web of
Sin series

KADER

The conference hall shimmered with the light from the oversized chandeliers. The atmosphere was set, the enticement dangling like a baited hook, and the gullible fish swimming about, ready to open wide while the sharks lurked in the depths.

I didn't belong here, that sentiment as obvious to me as to the others in my presence.

I wasn't an eager fish, willing to follow the school wherever the masses led.

Extending the analogy, I also wasn't a fisherman.

I was a hunter, standing motionless in knee-deep water, spear in hand, ready for the kill. Bring on the sharks. I was ready for them to show me their rows of teeth.

Dressing in a custom suit, shaving my face, and taming my hair didn't hide the truth beneath. All around me, the prey sensed the danger. A formal announcement of my presence or boast of my wealth, power, and abilities wasn't necessary. As one who truly possessed all three, the declaration preceded me, coming in silent waves radiating through the air and transmitted wordlessly.

One by one, fellow attendees moved about me, glasses of champagne in hand and their eyes averted, unable or unwilling to meet my gaze. Their only outward acknowledgments that they'd had an encounter with me were their whispers and mumbles as they uttered meaningless apologies under their breath.

"Excuse me."

"Sorry."

I didn't respond. There was no need to leave memories of my attendance other than a passing shadow.

The suit I'd worn was meant to allow me to fade into the crowd. In reality it showcased the gaping difference. My custom designer original was crème brûlée amongst a tray of Twinkies—lobster amid fast food.

Many of the people in this banquet hall were here to add their names to research, research few of them came close to understanding. Their riches were primarily on paper, their names listed in *Forbes* magazine for the world to lay prostrate at their feet. The truly wealthy didn't require a magazine to substantiate their worth. With our riches spread throughout the world, we did our best to keep its presence beneath the radar.

Scanning the faces of the invited guests, their attempts of

deception and pretense were as clear as a neon sign. This room was filled with impostors consumed by the need to fulfill their lackluster lives—lives devoid of true accomplishment—with the praises of those their money can buy.

Money—in most cases it wasn't an asset but the expandable depth of their credit.

Acknowledgments.

Recognition.

Their names on a plaque.

I had no more desire to fit in with these imitations of wealth than to dine on the cheap catering being offered or consume the basement-bottom bourbon in my hand.

Fitting in wasn't my thing or my goal.

I was here for one reason.

An assignment.

A job I agreed to fulfill.

Offers came and went.

I only took the assignments I wanted.

The decision was always mine.

I worked for no man but myself, on my schedule, as I saw fit.

My work had made me a wealthy man, taking me into the shadows and leaving me in the dark. Rarely did I accept an offer that brought me into the light.

However, even I could make an exception.

There was something about this assignment, this target...something that superseded my usual rules. I didn't need the money. I could spend the rest of my life hidden away on my ranch or sailing the seven seas. I vastly preferred my own company to those currently in my presence.

The door near the back of the room opened as more guests arrived.

I stood taller, taking her in.

She had arrived.

My *exception*.

She was the reason I was here.

At the sight of her, the small hairs on the back of my neck stood to attention. It was as if she was electricity and I was the rod. My reaction was visceral, much as it had been the first time I'd seen her.

The first time wasn't in person. It was her likeness that appeared on my computer screen and inexplicably, I was mesmerized. Her blue eyes stared at the camera, staring at me through the screen—seeing me in a way that even I was incapable of doing.

That thought was ludicrous and I knew it. Nevertheless, I was drawn.

As she accepted a glass of champagne, her head turned my direction. Instinctively, I took a step back, away from her gaze and into the shadows. I wasn't ready to meet those blue eyes in person, not yet. From the distance, I watched as I took in each inch of her.

A natural beauty, she seemed unaware of her effect on the men around her. Unlike her usual hairstyle, currently her dark hair was pulled up on the sides, the front styled in sweeping waves as long curls cascaded to the middle of her back. The softness of the style showcased her sensual neck and the simple pearl necklace. Under the lights from above, her gaze shone and lower lip disappeared as she nervously scanned the crowd.

The long black dress she wore hugged her breasts perfectly, yet the skirt flared outward, hiding what I knew was a beautifully curved body beneath. I'd done my research, bided my time. No, I hadn't seen her as up close as I desired; however, I'd observed. Despite the cool spring weather, at least three times a week she'd don skintight athletic apparel and run a local trail.

From my observation, Dr. Laurel Carlson wasn't a woman who thrived on being the center of attention—not like the room of potential donors, many vying for her attention. Her unease was evident in the lines around her eyes and the straightness of her neck. And yet still she was here, a testament to her dedication to this project.

If only I'd moved faster, done my job, this would have been avoided.

I hadn't. I'd been too enthralled in a way I found unusual yet fascinating. It was a twisted, gnawing feeling I didn't recognize.

I wanted to understand it.

In that search for comprehension, I'd taken too long.

Now, the stage was set for this show, and it was too late to lower the curtain.

For that, I was responsible.

Now was the time to move.

I leaned against the far wall, yet my mind stayed on her—my exception, the one who fascinated me in a different way.

Maybe it was more than her outward appearance. It was her intellect along with her doctorate in pharmacology—she also had a doctorate in applied mathematics with a focus on computational neuroscience and pharmacology. The combination intrigued me. Rarely did I encounter a woman like her. Most were different, satisfied to be a physical outlet for me or other men. They concentrated on appearance, keeping their knowledge level hidden. Admittedly, my sample was skewed. I paid those women for their services, thus reducing the variables.

Laurel was different; she was unaware of her beauty and unapologetically confident with her intelligence.

Despite my obvious fascination, she was my assignment.

I'd never failed at a job.

In that regard, Dr. Laurel Carlson wouldn't be my exception.

It was time to get this done.

LAUREL

The champagne's bubbles tickled my nose as I sipped the sweet liquid, hoping the alcohol would lessen my nerves. The banquet hall around me was filling with people as more joined the festivities by the minute. It wasn't your normal celebration—a wedding or party. No, tonight was a reception for potential investors. While that had been the intent stated on the invitations, in my mind we were essentially gathered for an auction.

As much as I didn't like the thought, in a way I was up for sale.

This wasn't some illicit sex auction.

If it were, it might be easier. One and done. Thank you very much.

My virtue wasn't up for sale.

It was my life's work that was on the block.

These people gathering around the banquet hall were potential investors willing to finance the continuation of my research—our research. I looked about the room of handsomely dressed people for my research partner, Russell Cartwright. If he were wearing his customary jeans and collared shirt covered by a lab coat, I'd be able to identify him immediately. There weren't any jeans or lab coats in here.

This was black tie.

The crowd was diverse, being brought together for this opportunity by Dr. Olsen, the dean of our research facility and Dr. Oaks, the dean of the university. Eric Olsen shared the guest list that included pharmaceutical representatives, wealthy businessmen and –women, entrepreneurs, and well-known alumni. As I scanned the room, I noted there were some people I knew, others I recognized, and many I'd never seen.

Dr. Russell Cartwright and I were here to hobnob with the people who had the opportunity to take our research to the next level. The money represented by these individuals could finance our future while easing ours and the university's growing concern over cost.

"Dr. Carlson," Stephanie, my assistant, whispered in my ear, pulling me from my thoughts.

Taking a step back, my cheeks rose and lips curled into a smile as I took in her appearance. A few years younger than I, she looked lovely in her long silver gown, one that brushed the tops of her high-heeled shoes. "Remind me to tell you how nice you looked tonight," I said.

"Thank you. You too. It's unusual to see everyone so formal."

My gaze continued its trek about the room. From custom suits to tuxedos, each man wore a shade of black or dark gray, their shoulders broad or stooped depending on their age and fitness level. The women were much more vibrant with dresses of all lengths in a rainbow of colors. The ladies' hairstyles varied, and the shades ranged from unnatural shades of pink and purple all the way to a lovely white. It seemed that this gathering drew people of all ages.

Stephanie was right—this wasn't our normal attire. I took a deep breath, the bodice of my gown hugging my breasts as the length of my black gown flowed to the floor. It was flattering yet not too revealing. Heaven knew, I would have never found a dress like this on my own. As someone who spent her days in a lab coat, dressing up for an occasion such as this wasn't my forte. No, I owed my current appearance to the lady at my side. She even arranged a hair appointment. I felt like I was in a scene from the old movie *Legally Blonde* or perhaps *My Fair Lady*. All I needed was a small dog and blonde hair or an English accent to perfect the part.

Schmoozing people wasn't my area of expertise either.

Asking for money was what people like Dr. Eric Olsen did best.

I worked better behind the scenes, more comfortable in tennis shoes, jeans, and a lab coat with my hair pulled back into a bun or ponytail, working scientific equations and observing physiological responses.

"Dr. Olsen would like you and Dr. Cartwright..." Stephanie said.

Though she was speaking, my attention was drawn to Russ. He was standing in a circle with a group of individuals, drinks in hand, speaking. I imagined him doing his best to avoid rolling his eyes. One of his pet peeves was discussing our research, simplifying it while staying vague. If I were closer to him, I might nudge him in the side to keep his eyes in place.

"Dr. Carlson," Stephanie said again, refocusing my attention on her. "As I was saying, Dr. Olsen would like you and Dr. Cartwright to join him by the podium as he greets the guests."

I sucked in a breath. "Tell me he doesn't expect us to speak."

I'd taken my position at the university to concentrate on research, not to teach large lecture halls of students. I negotiated for small discussion groups with doctoral students. Rarely did I facilitate studies for more than three or four students at a time. I strived to keep public speaking to a minimum.

Her eyes opened wide. "If he does, he's responsible for the outcome. You've told him a thousand different times that you prefer to stay out of the spotlight."

"Then why am I going up there?"

"Because he wants to put faces with the research." She grinned. "And most importantly because he's the dean."

She was right. It was that simple. I was here to put my face with the research, and he was my boss. That was why I would do as he asked. It was why I was here instead of in the lab or at home wrapped in a blanket with my Kindle.

Letting out my breath, I handed my glass of champagne to Stephanie. "Would you please hold this for me? I'll be so nervous in front of all of these people. If I take it up there, with my hands trembling, I'll probably spill it all over my dress."

Her smile bloomed as she reached for the glass. "Then hand it over. You look too nice to spill. And there's nothing to be nervous about. You and Dr. Cartwright should be the faces of this formula and resulting compound. You've done all the work."

I let out a sigh. "Thank you, Steph. You're a lifesaver."

"You keep concentrating on neurotransmitters and leave the fashion and wine-holding to me."

As I nodded, the chatter that had filled the room a moment ago began to quiet as Dr. Olsen stepped up to the podium in the front of the room.

"Deal," I whispered as I took a step forward.

"May I accompany you, Doctor?" Russell Cartwright, my co-scientist and the man who had worked beside me for the last four years, asked with a grin.

"You know how much I love this?" I whispered.

"About as much as I do. Keep smiling and we'll make a run for it as soon as we can."

Nodding, I looked down to see Russ's elbow bent, waiting for my hand to land gently upon it. "Thank you," I whispered, reaching for his arm. "I imagined tripping on the way to the front of the room."

A low laugh rumbled from his throat. "Laurel, I know you. That isn't too farfetched. I'm here to help convince these donors that what you lack in grace and coordination, you make up for in brains and determination." His steps paused as he looked my way. His brown eyes opened wider as he took in my appearance. "And beauty. You clean up very nice."

I smiled and did as he had done to me. Russ was wearing a dark suit, his top button of the jacket closed. The cut was tapered to accentuate his trim build. He'd shaved his usual dark five o'clock shadow at the urging of Dr. Olsen, leaving his cheeks smooth. His usually tousled hair was combed and in place. At a little over five feet, eight inches, Russ wasn't a tall man, but he was fit. I knew for a fact he visited the gym every morning before work. "Thank you, Russell. You don't look so bad yourself." We again continued walking through the crowd.

As Russ laughed at my compliment, my heels stuttered on the shiny floor and my fingers gripped Russ's arm tighter. My shuffle wasn't caused by lack of coordination. It was brought on by the strange sensation snaking through me as my gaze caught the stare of a man leaning casually against the back wall.

I couldn't place his name. Though vaguely familiar as if I'd seen him in a dream or perhaps on television, the reality was out of my grasp. There was something about him.

My taking notice of him didn't avert his stare.

With him looking directly at me, my pulse kicked up a notch.

I might not have noticed him if Russ hadn't detoured our path to avoid a gathering of people. Or maybe I would have.

Fate.

As our stares locked, I found myself unable to look away. My gaze was pulled to him as if by an external force—a magnet too powerful to fight.

Though he was at least fifty feet away, in that moment, he was all I saw.

I didn't know this man, his name or anything about him. Yet his eyes on me caused my skin to heat while at the same time, a chill to settle over me and my insides to twist.

The feeling was indescribable.

Was it...

Dread?

Attraction?

Curiosity?

Fear?

Excitement?

As his posture straightened, it was clear that he saw me too. More than saw, he was watching my every move.

From the distance and in the banquet room's lighting, his eyes appeared dark or perhaps that was a better description of his expression.

Shaking my head, I blinked and forced my eyes to turn away.

"Laurel..." Russ placed his hand over mine. "It'll be fine. If Dr. Olsen wants us to speak, I'll do it."

"What?" I asked, turning back to Russ as he continued to guide us forward.

Dr. Olsen had begun speaking though the words weren't registering. My mind was consumed with that man I didn't know.

I turned back over my shoulder, searching the spot where he'd been. As if evaporated, he was gone.

Was he in my imagination?

No, from the twisting of my insides, I knew he was real.

Who was he?

LAUREL

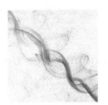

Standing dutifully to one side of Dr. Olsen while Russ stood on the other, we were on display. My thoughts of an auction returned. I'd probably read too many dark romance novels; nevertheless, that didn't stop the degrading thought from recurring. I tried to think of something else.

The image of the man with the intense stare materialized in my mind.

Who was he?

Was he watching us now?

Why did I care?

My cheeks heated as every eye in the room stared our way.

Dr. Olsen continued speaking about the strides we'd made in our research, bringing my thoughts away from the man and to my life's work. What he was saying and how much he could say made his speech a bit tricky. Both Russ and I had gone over and over it with him. There were details of what we were doing and what we'd discovered that were classified. Some of the people in this room represented rival facilities. He could speak in generalities, not specifics.

It was a fine line that he was walking, asking for money while keeping details covert. It wasn't like Dr. Olsen could guarantee that our compound would suppress the occurrence of traumatic memories while not debilitating the fight-or-flight impulse.

We weren't quite there.

The ability to make that statement was what we strived to accomplish and were closer than ever before. Once refined and verified, we believed our compound could be revolutionary. Potentially it could change psychiatric care for post-traumatic-stress disorder—PTSD—as we knew it while allowing patients who'd suffered traumatic experiences to live a normal, unhaunted existence.

Claiming that we'd achieved the final results wasn't yet possible. First we had to continue our research and gather additional clinical data. Currently the varying effects were too uncertain to go to press with the details. The reason for this gathering was to cultivate funding that could take us into the future to the next stage.

Getting from theory to reality took a great deal of money. Over the last few years we'd spent a significant amount. The university operated within limited budgets, and ours was busting at the seams.

The institutional review board had demands. Expanded clinical trials required additional faculty. Beyond the university, there were federal regulations that needed to be satisfied. We needed help.

Recently we'd experienced some unexpected and conflicting results that needed to be addressed. Everything required additional funding.

The people in this room—the ones staring at us—had the capital, and according to Dr. Olsen, we needed to play nice to get what we could.

"Dr. Carlson, could you answer that for us?"

Dr. Olsen's use of my name pulled me from my thoughts. The warmth of the lights shining our direction added to my unease. Like a student caught daydreaming by the professor, I was trapped. I hadn't been listening and had no idea what he wanted me to answer. Besides thinking about the limitations on what we could say about our research, I'd been scanning the room for the man I'd seen earlier.

With a feigned smile, I turned to our dean. "I'd like to be sure I heard the question correctly. Could you please repeat it?"

The already quiet room grew pin-drop silent as Dr. Olsen reached for the microphone. "Mr. Sinclair from Sinclair Pharmaceuticals..." He gestured toward the man in the front of the room. "...asked how long it would be before the compound was ready for patent."

My eyes grew wide as he spoke, vowing on the inside to tell Dr. Olsen exactly what I thought of him putting me on the spot. This was his show. We'd told him what to say. I considered turning toward Russ and letting him save me, but I wouldn't do that either. This question had come to me. I knew the most about this project.

Nerves be damned.

I looked to the man in front of the platform.

I'd mentioned the presence of rivals. From what we'd been told, Sinclair Pharmaceuticals was one of the biggest. They have been doing similar research. Word was that they weren't as advanced in their findings as we were. They weren't ready for clinical trials. It was no secret that they wanted our formula and had been after it for years, trying to beat us to patent.

We were winning. Which begged the question, why had Dr. Olsen invited Damien Sinclair to this gathering?

As I looked up to the entire audience, I took a breath, steeled my shoulders, and began, "As most of you are aware, the patent process is lengthy. We have more verification that needs to be done before we're ready to take that step."

"A year?" Mr. Sinclair asked.

"Sir, it's difficult to—"

"Two years?" he asked again. Turning to the rest of the room, he continued, "How much money do you suppose would be needed to fund research with no definite timeline?"

"Mr. Sinclair, we have a timeline," I said, my neck straightening. The crowd before me was beginning to murmur.

"It doesn't—" Mr. Sinclair's speech stopped midsentence as the man I'd seen in the back of the room stepped forward and turned to the crowd.

Dressed all in black, from his custom suit to his silk shirt, he stood inches taller than Mr. Sinclair. His sheer size warranted the quieting of the room. The raising of his hand finalized his unspoken request.

My breathing stammered as he turned my way.

I'd been wrong about his eyes when I thought they were dark. Instead, they were an intense green, and under the lights they shimmered with a golden hue. Though their color wasn't dark, his expression was—penetrating, even overpowering. I wasn't the only one who felt it. With a look alone, he'd rendered Mr. Sinclair speechless.

"Ladies and gentlemen," the mystery man said, "I would like to hear more from Dr. Olsen as I am sure you would also. The time for discussing specifics will come. If I am to invest in this interesting and promising endeavor, I would prefer to keep the public information to a minimum..." He turned to Mr. Sinclair. "...and confidential. I'm sure you would agree. Dr. Carlson is understandably limited on what she can say. I for one am vastly interested. If you're not, the speech can stop now." His gaze went to me. "I propose a solitary offer to fund Dr. Carlson and Dr. Cartwright's research."

The murmuring resumed.

"What? No," Mr. Sinclair said. "Sinclair Pharmaceuticals is not interested in stepping away. I simply wanted..."

The murmuring grew louder with more people voicing their interest in financing our continued research.

The stone-like features of my mystery man turned back toward the crowd as he once again lifted his hand. As he did, the cuff of his expensive jacket and black shirt donned with sparkling cufflinks moved, revealing his wrist adorned with colorful ink. "Then let them say what we came to hear without interruption."

This man appeared refined on the outside.

Yet the peek beneath his cuff revealed that his exterior was simply a cover or mask.

What was he like beneath that expensive suit?

Swallowing, I reached for the microphone. "Thank you, sir. As I was saying, our timetable is set, in principle. In reality it is fluid. We'll take the time necessary to ensure our data is correct and we have a clear path to patent." I turned to Dr. Olsen. "Dean Olsen, I believe the floor is again yours."

As I stepped back, I reached for my own hand, determined not to show that I was trembling.

It wasn't simply the fact I'd been called on to speak in front of this crowd of potential investors.

It was more than that.

There was something about the man with the green-eyed stare, hidden tattoo, and chiseled jaw that twisted at my insides, gnawing away at my nerves and leaving them bare for the room to see.

I replayed the scene. Through it all, the exchange with

Mr. Sinclair and everything, the mystery man remained eerily calm.

In our line of research, I was an expert at interpreting emotions, watching and seeing outward signs that others didn't notice.

Perspiration on the lip.

Clenching of the jaw.

Bulging of muscles on extremities.

Fisting of fingers.

Increased respiration.

Flaring of nostrils.

Some of those signs had been exhibited by Damien Sinclair but not by the stranger.

I continued to watch the mystery man. With confidence in his step, he disappeared into the crowd. His broad shoulders and short light-brown ponytail were the last I saw of him as the bright lights pointing our direction veiled the back of the room in shadows.

Despite the inability to see into the darkness, my gaze continued to search, mysteriously drawn to him in a way I'd never before known.

No, there was once, long ago.

That person was gone. And yet this was the same feeling.

It had been too long since I'd last seen the only man who'd owned a piece of my heart, soul, and body. Truly he'd been a boy. We were merely kids when we parted, though at the time we'd thought we were worldly.

My childhood in Chicago was gone. That was a lifetime ago.

All I knew with one hundred percent certainty was that the man who had caught my attention and twisted my mind and body couldn't be the same one I'd known. The man who'd just spoken was not a ghost. He was alive, powerful, and for some reason, had come to my rescue and earned my attention.

KADER

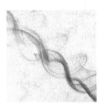

$\mathcal{M}$y molars strained under the pressure.

The presence of an unusual physical response was the catalyst.

I was off my game—out of my head.

"Fuck!" The sentiment ran on repeat in my head as other guests averted their gazes and wisely stepped aside, once again clearing a path for my return to the shadows.

My job worked for me because somewhere along the way, somewhere in my life, I'd faced the devil and returned victorious. The gates of hell had been opened to me and instead of entering, I walked away.

While metaphoric, the result was the same.

I'd faced what others feared and I survived.

Because of that experience, nothing frightened me. Nothing excited me. I lived and worked by my own rules, finding satisfaction in ways others may find discontent or even repulsion.

What pleased me?

A job well done.

A security system breached.

A stock split.

A kill shot from two thousand meters.

The sound of bones breaking under pressure.

The knowledge that I held the power of life and death.

I supposed that *success* was what brought me the closest thing to pleasure I could obtain.

Women?

Sometimes.

Success brought money.

Money delivered anything.

A warm, willing fuck was no exception.

Don't ask me their names or even what they looked like—blonde, brunette, or redhead. My preference centered more on availability and willingness to abide by my rules.

That wasn't a problem for the women who took the payout. Few saw my face.

Though my entire appearance had been altered, I had my anonymity to maintain.

Blindfolds were not used for kink but for survival.

And even if one saw, she never learned my name, never met my gaze. The name I'd had before Satan bid my entrance to hell was gone.

A dead man.

Signed, sealed, and certified.

Thank you, Uncle Sam.

I had a new name.

My reputation was built in places decent people didn't frequent. The dark web was layered. If you were capable of finding me, I now respond to one name—Kader.

Rebirth as an adult had its advantages. One was the ability to choose my own name.

Kader had special significance to me, meaning destiny in Turkish.

That was my job now—determining people's destiny.

Tonight I'd crossed a line I rarely approached.

I'd made an exception—again.

Why the fuck would I go to Laurel's rescue?

She didn't need it.

Her curriculum vitae was filled with a long list of academic accomplishments.

She was more than capable of coming to her own verbal defense. And yet something about her brought to life a protective streak deep inside me, one I'd never before known existed.

There was a reason.

She'd looked at me from across the room. Her blue eyes didn't shy away.

That was no excuse for bringing myself into the spotlight.

My anger wasn't at her. It was at me.

This was oddly unusual.

Emotion in general was beyond my psychological ability.

I got results.

"Fuck."

My speaking to a room of people in the light was reckless and out of character.

I'd let this assignment go on too long.

My message would be delivered tonight.

Not to a room of faces.

To one person.

I'd give her one more chance to turn those blue eyes away.

LAUREL

"**W**ho was that man?" Stephanie asked as she met me after Dr. Olsen's greeting.

Taking the glass of champagne, I raised it to my lips and emptied the contents.

"Whoa," she said with a grin.

"I don't know who he was. I didn't recognize him."

Stephanie exaggerated a shiver. "There was something about him that felt—well, he gave me the creeps."

My eyes widened. That was the exact opposite from my reaction.

Before I could respond, she went on, "I checked everyone's online profiles to help you with names if you needed it."

"You know I need it," I said with a giggle.

A giggle?

I don't giggle.

"Oh, maybe I drank that champagne a bit fast."

"You think?"

I reached for her arm and steadied myself. "I need a few minutes. Between the heat of the lights and everyone staring up there, I'm a bit wobbly."

Right, Laurel. It had nothing to do with that man, the way he was looking at you, or the glass of bubbly you just downed in two seconds flat.

"There's a ladies' lounge out the door and down the hallway to the right. Would you like me to get you something? Water maybe?"

I smiled her way. "I would just like to sit for a minute before I have to talk to anyone else."

"Do you want me to go with you?" Stephanie asked.

"No, I'll be fine. If they ask, please let Drs. Olsen and Cartwright know I'll be right back."

The room was set for talking with a splattering of tall tables without chairs. There were also a few larger round tables with chairs near the back. Along one side wall was a buffet table filled with appetizers and hors d'oeuvres, and on the other side of the room was a full bar. I could sit at one of the large tables near the back, but that would lead to people.

A moment alone in the ladies' lounge sounded like a better idea.

As I nodded at people that I passed, an idea came to mind. Maybe I could hide in the lounge for the rest of the night. It was a good thought except it wouldn't work, and it wouldn't be fair to Russ.

I began weaving around people, getting closer to the door. As I did, I couldn't help but search for the man from earlier. I wasn't certain why I was searching; however, based on the speed at which my pulse thumped through my veins, I wanted another visual confirmation.

What would I do if I found him?

Go up and talk to him—ask him who he was?

I doubted it.

I suspected that if we were to be face-to-face, the words I wanted to say wouldn't come any easier than they had up on the stage. Maybe I simply wanted to know his location—a place to avoid.

"Dr. Carlson."

"Dr. Carlson?"

My name came from all directions, yet I only continued nodding as I made my way through the crowd, closer to the doorway. Once there, I pushed the large door open and stepped from the banquet hall.

As soon as the door closed behind me, a calming sensation washed over me. To my relief there weren't any other activities in this part of the convention center. At the far end of the hallway a group of people had gathered. Yet thankfully, my path was clear—not another soul between me and the ladies' lounge.

With each step, I soaked in the silence of my new surroundings. The temperature out here was easily ten degrees cooler and the noise level many decibels quieter than the banquet hall. After Dr. Olsen's speech, the room had come to life, buzzing with conversations. My steps steadied as I moved closer to the ladies' lounge.

Would the ladies' lounge provide me with the momentary isolation I desired?

I stopped short of the lounge and pulled on the handle to an unused banquet hall. With only the light from the exit sign, I scanned the vacant room. It was set for an impending event, the tables holding centerpieces of fresh flowers. Near the door was a large floral arrangement beside a sign on an easel. Even in the dim lighting I could read the bride's and groom's names.

"Congratulations, Mr. and Mrs. Miller," I whispered.

Being it was Friday night, I could assume the nuptials would take place tomorrow.

I took a deep breath.

Yes, this would give me a moment of much-needed seclusion.

I pulled out a chair from one of the first tables, careful not to disturb the decor. The aroma of gardenias and jasmine hung in the air, sweet yet not overpowering. Taking another deep breath, I slowly released it. A few more times and the internal thumping of my circulation faded to its normal cadence. Sighing, I closed my eyes.

If I could make a wish and it be granted, I'd no longer be at the convention center dressed up like a prized pig for the fair. No, I'd be home on my own sofa with soft music and my Kindle, perhaps even a glass of wine. The idea made my cheeks rise as my lips turned upward.

"Another few hours and you'll be there," I silently reassured myself.

With my eyes closed, my thoughts went to the place they'd been since I first saw him—back to the man in the banquet hall. Though I'd watched him walk through the crowd, I hadn't been able to spot him after Dr. Olsen's greeting. I recalled what he'd said when he interrupted Mr. Sinclair. The mystery man had said he would propose a solitary deal for financing our research. Surely he didn't comprehend the amount of funding we were seeking.

There was something else—something about his stare.

I startled as the distinctive click of a locking mechanism echoed through the empty hall, the scent of blossoming flowers now mixed with rich masculine-scented cologne, heavy in birch and black-currant spices.

Sucking in a breath, my eyes opened, and I spun toward the door. In the low light of the sign was the man in my thoughts. The mystery man from the banquet hall was here. My mind couldn't process, couldn't put the pieces together.

"May I help you?" I asked.

Why had I gone into an empty room?

My gaze searched around him. The door behind him to the hallway was closed as it had been.

Was it now locked?

Standing, I tried to appear confident, as if this man didn't intrigue me.

Instead of answering, he took another step my direction.

My pulse kicked up a notch as he continued his silent stare.

"What do you want?"

With each of his steps forward I found myself backing away. Granted, it didn't scream confidence, but it did keep him at an even distance. That was, until my shoulders collided with a side wall.

Panic began to percolate in my stomach, leaching its way through my veins. There was something unsettling about the man before me. He barely blinked, his gaze fixed upon me. I looked down, following his stare and becoming suddenly self-conscious of the gown and the way the neckline flattered my breasts.

Where was my lab coat when I needed it?

"Sir, I believe this room is not meant for our event. We should leave." All the while I continued to scan him up and down. He was even taller than he'd appeared from a distance.

Larger than life, his presence dominated even this empty room.

Though I wanted to appear calm, my physiological response to his presence was involuntary. Shallow breathing, trembling, fisted hands, and thumping pulse—I was the clinical example of fight-or-flight.

Given the choice, I would choose flight.

I moved along the wall, my high heels scooting as I snaked toward the door.

Blocked by a tray upon a stand filled with coffee cups, my choices were limited.

With the mountain of a man between me and a locked door, flight wasn't a viable option.

That left fight.

No.

There was no way. He was too large. Physically, I wouldn't stand a chance.

Pepper spray.

Yes, I had it in my purse.

My eyes darted to the chair where I'd been sitting.

Shit.

I didn't have my purse.

Straightening my shoulders, I met his stare. "Neither of us should be here," I said, summoning all the authority that I could muster.

He remained still as if my words held no meaning. From his reaction, or should I say lack thereof, I couldn't be sure that he'd heard me.

Had I spoken aloud?

Could he hear?

Was he deaf?

No. He'd responded to Damien's questions. He could hear.

Without a word, the mystery man took one step closer and then another. His expensive loafers moved silently over the marble floor, barely tapping the surface. With each step nearer he grew, appearing larger than the second before.

Taller.

Broader.

If my vision were a camera's view, this man would now consume the entirety of the lens.

Swallowing, I refused to look away, continuing our silent battle of wills. I lifted my chin, unwilling to cower in fear. His cologne dominated my senses as much as his presence. Power and control radiated from him in a way I'd never before sensed.

I'd spent most of my adult life around academia. There were men and women with impressive credentials who ran departments and entire universities and yet their presence paled in comparison to this man's.

As we continued to stare, I sensed something hauntingly familiar about him, yet I knew that wasn't possible.

"Who are you and why are you here?" Maybe if I repeated my questions he would answer.

He stopped an arm's length away.

It might be a misinterpretation; however, the space he allowed me gave me a bit of confidence. I lifted my face higher. "If you come closer, I'll scream."

One side of his lips lifted slightly. "Dr. Carlson..." His deep voice rumbled through me like thunder on a cloudy day. "...if I wanted to harm you, you wouldn't be standing here."

"Then what do you want?"

He shook his head as he unashamedly scanned to my breasts and back to my eyes. "Things I shouldn't."

His answer prickled my skin. Still, I managed to respond, "You shouldn't be in here." With my mind churning with possibilities of his desires, apparently I thought that stating the obvious was important.

"Neither should you. It's not safe."

"I just..." I began my explanation and stopped. "Fine. Then move and I'll leave."

"Your formula," he said.

"What about it?"

"I want it. My employer wants it."

"Financial sponsorship should be discussed with Dr. Olsen."

He shook his head. The tendons in his neck strained as he spoke. "You misunderstand, Dr. Carlson. My employer doesn't want to finance your continued research. My employer wants to finance the discontinuation of your research. That same entity is willing to go to great lengths to procure all rights to your formula as it is today and insure that further public or private research ceases to continue. I'd advise you to take the deal. You'd be done with this little project and be a wealthy woman able to work on another project or perhaps never work another day in your life. That choice would be yours."

"What?" I tried to follow his words but they weren't making sense. "No, that isn't possible."

"It beats the alternative, Doctor. Take the offer. No matter what you decide, the research is over."

"It isn't over. We're too close. You don't know what you're talking about."

"Again, you're mistaken. My employer knows all about

your formula and the compound's potential as well as more dubious uses. Think of this as an offer you can't refuse."

"Drs. Cartwright and Olsen—"

"May not know about this offer—for their safety."

"This is ludicrous." I pointed toward the door. "There's an entire room of people that know what we're doing. It can't just stop."

"What is your price, Dr. Carlson? How much?" His green gaze scanned me up and down.

"I'm not for sale."

This time both sides of his lips moved upward. "Shame really. If you were on the auction block, I'd double the highest offer."

"What?"

"Everyone has a price, Doctor, which means everyone is for sale." His lips flattened for a second before continuing. "Right now, we're talking about your work. If the offer includes you, I may have to join the bidding."

I didn't know if I should be appalled by his insinuation or flattered. Either way, his words affected me in a way I didn't recognize.

As he reached into his jacket, I gasped, flattening myself against the wall, suspecting he was reaching for a gun or something equally as nefarious. Instead, he removed a business card and handed it my direction.

Apprehensively, I reached out, seizing the card.

The surface was black, and on the front was gold-foil embossed lettering. Truly it wasn't lettering. There were no words, only a ten-digit number. I turned it over. The back side was also black.

"That number can't be traced," he said, "so don't even try. I'll expect a call from you within the week with your price. Think about it. Think about your parents in Iowa and your sister and niece in Illinois. What could you do for them with an untold amount of money?"

"No, this doesn't make any sense. I don't own the formula. The university does."

"You know what it contains. No one knows it as well as you."

"But I can't—"

"Today is Friday. One week, Dr. Carlson. Tell no one. I can't be held responsible for what may happen if you do."

After his last word, he turned toward the door, showing me the same view I'd seen as he disappeared into the crowd earlier in the evening.

"Wait," I exclaimed. He'd mentioned my family.

Was his last statement a threat?

When he turned back to me, I asked, "How do you know about my family?"

"I know everything about you, Laurel. One week."

Without another word, he twisted the large lock on the door and after opening it, stepped into the hallway. For a moment I stood staring at the number on the card. The area code was local. There had to be a way to find out where it went.

I needed more information. Pushing the card into the

pocket of my dress, I rushed out of the empty banquet hall, following his steps. I peered both directions. The hallway was empty save for a lone convention center employee standing near the doors to the banquet hall filled with people waiting for my return. His head was down, his phone in hand.

Going to him, I asked, "Excuse me?"

"Yes, ma'am," the young man replied, looking away from the screen.

"Which way did that man go?"

He shook his head. "I didn't see a man."

I lifted my hand. "Tall, wearing a dark suit. Big, not fat —intimidating."

"No. No one like that. I'd remember someone like that."

LAUREL

$\mathcal{M}$y steps faltered as I stood outside the door to the gathering within.

What had just happened?

This wasn't real life. Encounters like that didn't happen.

Did they?

Perhaps it had been a dream.

Or maybe I'd just been inside a scene of some parallel-universe psychological thriller. If that were the case, I wanted to change the channel and forget it had happened.

Abandon my research?

No, hell no.

There wasn't a price that would make me do that. It was like the commercial for the credit card—continuing our research was *priceless*.

I took a deep breath as my hand rested upon the large handle.

Could I do this, move forward as if that encounter hadn't happened?

I didn't have a choice. There was a room full of people waiting for me.

What if I went straight to Eric Olsen or Russ Cartwright and told them what had happened? I wasn't convinced they'd believe me. To be honest, I was having difficulty believing it.

I put my hand into my pocket and let my fingers skim over the gold-foil numbers on the black card. Pulling it out, I stared again at the number.

The card was real.

The numbers were real.

That meant the encounter had been real too.

Taking a deep breath, I pulled the large door toward me and stuffed the card back into my pocket. The interior of the banquet hall was as it had been when I'd stepped out. If anything had changed, it was that the noise level of conversation increased. As I scanned the crowd, most with glasses in hand, I credited the alcohol with the volume. According to Eric, it was supposed to do more than loosen tongues; it was also supposed to loosen wallets.

In today's world, a simple app could be used. No real money changed hands. As I searched the crowd, I fidgeted with the black card. Every man looked the same in their dark suits, yet none were the one I sought. The one I was searching for had disappeared.

"Dr. Carlson," Dr. Olsen said, coming toward me.

With my stomach churning, I pulled my hand from my pocket, leaving the card in place. As my dean came closer, I came to a conclusion. I was many things, none of which was a convincing actor.

I couldn't stay here. I needed to leave and call my family. I wouldn't tell them anything, just check on them, tell them I loved them and to be careful.

Eric Olsen stood close, his voice low. "I'm glad to see you. I was afraid you tried to sneak out early. Come with me. I have some investors who would love to speak with you."

"Eric, something has come up. I told you my reservations about this evening. We've already said too much."

He shook his head dismissively. "Laurel, the work you do is above their heads. They simply want to be involved in something revolutionary. We both know that no one here understands the pharmacology or physiology behind what you've accomplished. Just pacify them and they'll willingly contribute their funds."

"And say what?"

"Whatever they want to hear."

I looked up at Dr. Olsen. "Eric, what if we can't refine it. What if we're at a dead end?"

Dr. Olsen took a step back; his tone was hushed and reactionary. "Laurel, why would you say that?" His gaze flitted around us. "And here? What if you were overheard?"

"Fine," I said. "I'll play nice, but classified is still classified. People already know too much."

"Doctors," Damien Sinclair said, his deep voice interrupting our conversation.

"Mr. Sinclair," Dr. Olsen greeted.

Pasting on my 'play nice' smile, I repeated the greeting, a bit less enthusiastically than my dean. "Mr. Sinclair."

He offered his hand to Eric before turning to me. Proper manners caused my hand to also rise. Mr. Sinclair's grip was firm until he turned my hand over and bowed to brush his lips over my knuckles. My already-queasy stomach bubbled with bile as I retrieved my hand.

"Mr. Sinclair," I stated again.

"Now, now. Call me Damien. After all, it appears we'll be working on the same team. We should get to know one another." The ends of his thin lips turned upward. "Don't you agree, Laurel?"

Taller than I with blond hair and dark blue eyes, I would suppose many women found Damien Sinclair attractive. I wasn't one of them. His growing smile reminded me of a cartoon character who found pleasure in stealing other people's Christmas. "Is that how it appears, Mr. Sinclair?" I asked, purposely not using his first name. "From this perspective, I don't share the inevitability that you seem to foresee."

"It's just a matter of time. Think of the possibilities. You and Russell join us at Sinclair Pharmaceuticals and the university gets exclusive rights to the published research. We supply the needed funds and are therefore granted the patent. You are able to continue your research without the constraints of an institution and the institutional review board. You know they're going to fight you tooth and nail on the broader clinical trials."

How did he know about the smaller clinical trials? We hadn't released that information. Instead of confirming or denying, I said, "There are still regulations and standards that must be—"

"Mr. Sinclair," Dr. Olsen said, interrupting my rebuttal. "The university has already supplied—"

"Come on," Damien interrupted Eric, "if the university was behind you and your pet project, tonight's little pony show and campaign for financial backers wouldn't have happened." He reached for my arm.

My gaze went to his touch and back to him, fire hopefully shooting from my blue orbs. It must have worked for he removed his hand. I could only hope his fingertips were scorched.

"Laurel, I'd like to talk to you and Russ about this further. We're prepared to make both of you a substantial offer." He turned back to Eric. "Or we can go the route of financing a substantial portion and you stay with the constraints of the university. No matter the decision, we will obtain the information we seek, and eventually this drug will have the Sinclair moniker."

"I believe this conversation is over," Dr. Olsen said. "I was just about to escort Dr. Carlson to other potential investors. You see, Mr. Sinclair, nothing is set in stone."

As we stepped away, I whispered to Eric, "He mentioned expanded clinical trials. How could he know about the smaller ones in progress and why was he invited? They've been after this formula since it was theory."

Ignoring my first question, Eric answered my second. "He wasn't invited. He called in a favor to Dean Oaks."

Dean Oaks, the dean of the entire university, was ultimately the man everyone answered to. He also had final say in budgets. Our research needed time. It made sense that he'd want the biggest possible financial contributors to be present. And then I had another thought. "Did he invite anyone else?"

"Why do you ask?" However, before I could answer, the introductions were in progress with the new group of donors.

Did my mystery man have a connection with the dean of the university?

I had more questions than answers.

LAUREL

Though I desperately wanted to leave the convention center, I stayed, answering questions and doing my best to remain vague. The entire time my thoughts were all over the place—from the offer the man made in private to Damien Sinclair's offer. They both seemed to know more about our work than they should, more than had been released.

On numerous occasions, I considered telling Eric or Russ about the ludicrous encounter. Part of me hoped that if I shared it with them, they would dismiss it. I wanted both of my colleagues to tell me that it was farfetched and ridiculous. In reality, I was seeking the reassurance that I didn't feel.

Each time I thought to bring it up, the man's warning came back to me. He'd said that telling either of them would put them in danger.

Why had he come to me? Why not to Russ? Or had he? Had he propositioned both of us?

Due to the secrecy of our formula, neither Russ nor I nor the lab held complete files. We each maintained a portion of the data. Only when we were together did we have the full research. Because of that system, if I gave my information up to that man, it wouldn't be enough for his employer to duplicate it.

And then on my way home, it hit me.

My knuckles blanched as I tightened my grip on the steering wheel and navigated the night streets. My mind wasn't on the route I drove daily. It was concentrating on the fact that someone wanted to stop our research.

The man didn't need all of the data to make the research stop.

All it took was one half—me.

If I gave up my research that would be enough to bring everything to a screeching halt.

That was what he'd said was his employer's goal.

If my portion was missing, Russ would need to go back to the beginning.

Why did they want to stop it?

I continued to navigate the shiny streets as myriad thoughts swirled. Tall streetlights cast circles of illumination bringing the falling precipitation to sight. It was spring in Indiana and Mother Nature couldn't decide if she wanted snow, ice, or rain. The precipitation now dotting my windshield was a vague combination of all of the above, melting upon contact and giving the world a glossy sheen.

These were the road conditions that could catch drivers unaware. Lulled into a false sense of security, believing it was rain when all at once, the street would become slick and tires would lose their grip.

The surroundings darkened as I left the main streets and neared my neighborhood. Porch lights dotted the path, yet the tall posts were gone, replaced by hundred-year-old trees ready to sprout their new leaves. The naked branches created a canopy over the street as I made my way into my driveway and parked beside my home.

A cold breeze blew.

Pulling my jacket around me, I opened the car door as the sounds of rain and wind howled all around me. My high heels weren't meant for slippery conditions. Thankfully the driveway was more wet than slick. The long skirt of my dress quickly dotted with the falling moisture, as the wind twisted it about my legs, and I hurriedly made my way toward the side door to my home, thankfully covered by a small awning.

Shivering, I looked up at the darkened windows. I hadn't thought to leave a light on before I left. I'd been too concerned about the way the night would go.

I'd had no idea, no way to predict what actually happened.

Bang.

I gasped, my pulse once again spiking as the keys in my hand jingled and the storm door flew back against the house.

Startled, I reached for the glass door, almost dropping my keys to the concrete step.

Bang.

"Settle down," I said to myself. The recurring sound was a familiar happening most days and nights the wind blew. It was Mrs. Beeson's back gate, the one my neighbor often forgot to latch. I contemplated trekking into the backyard and latching it as I'd done many times. However, as I eyed the dark and shadowed yards and the rain continued to fall, I decided to let it be.

As for my storm door, the glider needed repair, one of the many items on my ever-present to-do list. That was what happened when one owned a century-old home.

I stepped into the house through the door that led to my kitchen. Renovated by the previous owners, it was small but modern, complete with stainless steel appliances and hard-surface countertops. With a flip of the light switch my world was brought into view. Checking the outside door, I closed and locked the large wooden door. Shivering, I removed my wet coat and inspected the damage to my dress.

I hadn't planned to wear it again, and by the looks of it, that was a good thing. My styled hair was ruined with locks no longer hanging in curls. No, they were dripping. Taking off the high heels, I sighed in relief as I carried them toward my bedroom. Each step over the old floor creaked as the wind continued to rattle the windowpanes.

When I reached the wooden staircase, I changed my mind, setting my shoes on the second step instead of going up to my room. Though I was anxious to get out of the wet dress and comb out my hair, I had something more pressing to do.

Back in the kitchen, I found my purse and took out my phone. My reflection in the old French doors that led to my patio was a far cry from the woman at the gathering. Nevertheless, this needed to be done. Doing what I'd been thinking about since my mysterious encounter, I went to the living room and settled on the sofa.

A quick glance at the clock told me that the time was after eleven. That was true here, but that also meant that it was an hour earlier in Iowa and Illinois. Searching my contacts, I found my parents' number and called them first.

My mother answered.

"Hi, Mom. It's Laurel."

"Laurel, is everything all right? It isn't like you to call this late."

"Did I wake you?"

"Of course not. You know we like to watch the news before going to bed."

I shook my head. Nowadays, most people got their news from apps on their phone. Not my parents. They're fervent viewers of morning, evening, and late-night local news programs and still subscribed to the local newspaper.

No matter how old-fashioned they were, it was good to hear my mom's voice, to know she was safe.

After an enlightening conversation about the plants she was growing in her greenhouse, I asked, "Hey, have you spoken to Ally lately?" Ally was my sister, two years older than I, and we used to be close.

"It's been a week, I think," she replied.

"How is Haley doing?" The man had mentioned my parents, my sister, and my niece. Haley was my five-year-old niece.

"She's been practicing for the spring concert at her school. Ally said she sings constantly, even in her sleep."

That made me smile. "Okay, I better let you go."

"Before you hang up, your dad wants to talk to you."

"Hi, sweetheart," my father's voice came through the phone before I could agree.

"Hi, Dad."

"Have you fixed that glider on your side door?"

I shook my head. "No, Dad. I've been busy at work."

"What about that man friend of yours."

"Russ is a friend, Dad. He is also busy at work."

"Well, I've been thinking about it. You need to get it fixed before spring storms hit. Otherwise, the wind can really—"

As if cued by a director, the screen door, the one I'd latched, slammed against the side of the house. The latch could use work too.

"I will, Dad," I said with a grin. I wouldn't do it soon, but if it made him feel better to think I would, I'd say it. "Hey, Dad?"

"Yes."

"You and Mom stay safe. Make sure the doors are locked."

"You know nothing happens out here in the country.

Nearly a decade out here and the only time we lock our doors is when we go out of town."

I knew that was the case. If the mystery man knew all about me, could he know that too? "Please, Dad?"

"Sure, sweetheart. We'll do that."

As we said our goodbyes, I wondered if his promise of locking doors was as sincere as mine to fix my side-door glider.

If that were the case, fixing the glider had just been moved up my to-do list.

The door slammed again.

Back in the kitchen, I stood near the wooden door.

How had the storm door opened?

Was the latch bad or had someone opened my door?

My skin grew warm and goose bumps formed as I peeked out the nearby window.

Darkness created a mirror, keeping my view of outside obscured.

No longer did I hear just the sound of the door; the old doorknob rattled.

I stepped away from the window, my heart rate accelerating. Opening my purse, still on the kitchen table, I removed the small canister of pepper spray.

Now, along with the rattling, there was pounding on the wooden door.

"Who is it?" I asked loudly.

"Laurel, it's me. Your lights are on. Let me in."

LAUREL

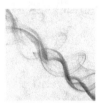

I let out a long breath as I willed my hands to stop shaking, tossed the pepper spray canister onto the kitchen table, and unlocked the door. My fear from seconds earlier evaporated, replaced with relief as I pulled the door inward and motioned for Russ to enter.

"What are you doing here?" I asked.

"I was worried about you."

The scent of his cologne mixed with whiskey hung around him like a cloud. I was momentarily reminded of the nameless man's cologne, richer and more masculine than the one Russ wore.

Stop thinking about him.

I let Russ's words sink in.

He was worried? Does he know about my encounter?

"You'll see me Monday. Besides we both had a few drinks. You should be home, not driving these wet streets."

Shaking the rain from himself and ignoring my veiled suggestion to leave, Russ draped his wet top coat on the back of another one of the kitchen chairs. "Your storm door needs to be fixed. The damn wind ripped it right out of my hands."

"Yeah," I said with a chuckle. "My dad thinks I should ask you to do it."

"I would, Laurel. I'd do more than that."

I inhaled. "I know, Russ. And I thank you. I'm capable of putting on a new glider. It's time that's the issue."

"Yeah, not a lot of that around anymore." He reached for a rogue strand of my hair and ran it between his fingers as a sad smile came to his lips. "Wouldn't it be nice?"

"What?"

"To have time."

Russ's and my relationship was more than strictly work and significantly less than a love affair. If I were to classify our relationship, I'd call it convenient and generally mutually beneficial.

Hours of togetherness day in and day out created a familiarity. Complicated conversations with endless discussion of theories and hypotheses often lasted into the night. Deadlines and reports constantly loomed omnipresent. Truly, our connection was more cerebral than emotional. The physical attraction was simply a byproduct of all of the above.

Over the years, Russ and I had found comfort in our similarities as well as enjoyment in a brief hiatus from over-thinking and the physiological relief that could ensue from our connections.

Was Russ the man I imagined for my soul mate?

No, that bar had been set too high when I was too young. Fulfilling the fantasy that was conjured in a young, impressionable mind was beyond obtainable. The green-eyed stare of a man whose name I didn't know came to mind.

That was what it was, I realized. His eyes reminded me of...

Stop it.

That wasn't possible. The mystery man held no other similarity.

Similar, not the same.

Then why settle for Russ?

I asked myself that same question more than once.

The answer that came to mind was that he was present.

He was real.

He had substance beyond the wistful illusions that the subconscious could conjure.

I took a step back. "Russ, it's late. I wish you would have called first before coming over."

Instead of taking my more direct hint to leave, Russ brushed past me and into the living room. With a sigh, he sat back on the couch, unbuttoned his suit coat, loosened his tie, and crossed one ankle over his knee. When he looked up at me his expression lingered between concern and desire. "You seemed off tonight. Was it because of Damien?"

As he waited for my answer, a new chill washed over me. I

wasn't certain if it came from Russ's question or my wet dress. Shaking my head, I did as I'd done most of the night and spoke in vague generalities. "Gatherings like that make me uncomfortable."

"I know that. It seemed like more."

If I couldn't end this conversation, at least I could postpone it. "Give me a second, please. I need to change out of this wet dress and put on something—"

"More comfortable." His cheeks rose and eyebrows danced as he attempted to finish my sentence. "I like the sound of that."

I didn't respond. Instead, turning away, I walked barefoot toward the stairs. Stepping onto the first step, I reached down and picked up my shoes, the ones I'd placed there earlier. When I stood straight, the warmth of Russ's body was behind me and his arms began to encircle my waist. Taking another step up and out of his reach, I turned to face him.

His eyes were glassy as he looked up at me from the step below. "Laurel, I know you don't like occasions like tonight. That doesn't mean you didn't knock them dead..." He ran the palm of his hand over my arm. "...absolutely stunning in this dress and quick on your feet with answers and explanations."

"Russ..."

"I'd be happy to help you change into something more comfortable or..." He reached for a stray lock of my hair. "...maybe a warm shower after being out in that freezing rain."

I shook my head. Although I liked the idea of not being

alone, I wasn't in the mood for what he proposed. My mind was too full of conflicting thoughts, most of them circling back to the man from the back of the room, the one who ambushed me, and the one I couldn't stop thinking about. "Not tonight. I'm bushed."

His chest inflated as he inhaled and deflated as he exhaled. With each breath the scent of whiskey returned.

"How much did you drink tonight?" I asked.

He shrugged. "I wasn't keeping count."

"Listen, I don't want you to drive home. You can stay here. I'll make you a bed on the couch."

Russ's head tilted as his jaw clenched. "Laurel, I wanted to talk to you about Sinclair Pharmaceuticals someplace without ears."

"So...not at work."

"We can talk here, but with our heads on a pillow would be another option."

There had been many nights we'd taken that option, continuing our work talk until we gave up and succumbed to sleep.

"There's nothing to talk about," I said. "The decision isn't ours. It's up to Eric if he accepts their money."

"Is it?" Russ asked. "Eric told me that Dean Oaks was the one who invited Damien."

"Yes, he told me the same thing."

Russ stepped back down to the floor and turned in a circle. "We've worked too damn hard for them to come in, take the credit." His eyes widened. "Damien had another offer, one to hire us, moving the research to Sinclair."

"I'm not for sale." I found it somewhat ironic that I'd repeated the same sentence twice in one night. When Russ just looked at me, I asked, "Do you have numbers? Did he make a specific offer?"

"Hell no," he said. "I told Damien to stick his offer up his ass. We weren't interested."

"Would you...?" I tugged on my upper lip, pulling it between my teeth. "I mean...is there a price that would make you sell."

"To Sinclair?"

I shrugged. "To anyone."

"Is there a price you'd sell?"

"I didn't think there was. Like you said, we've worked too hard and for too long. The potential for this drug is far-reaching. I want to be around to see it come to fruition."

He nodded. "Then we're on the same page. We'll tell Eric on Monday that our vote is for no."

"Damien essentially offered me a job in front of Eric," I said. "I think we should make it clear to Eric and Damien that neither of us have any intentions of jumping ship." I continued, thinking out loud, "I mean, I'm sure Eric's worried. He knows the university can't possibly offer us the kind of money Sinclair would offer."

"I agree. We'll tell him where we stand and let him handle Dr. Oaks." Russ reached for my hand, the one on the banister. "I'll see you Monday."

"You don't have to go."

"I do because if I stay here, I won't stay on that couch."

"Good night, Russ. Drive carefully."

He turned to walk away.

"Russ?"

"Yeah, Laurel?"

"Text me when you get to your place, please?" I didn't want to sleep with him; however, I wanted to be sure he was safe. My offer of the couch was real. Yes, there was a spare room upstairs, but I knew him. I knew me. Distance was the best way to stay true to my decision.

His lips curled into a sad smile. "Sure, I'll send a text."

For a moment, we stood in silence.

Russ tilted his head. "We're good. This..." He motioned between us. "...we agreed it didn't interfere with our work."

"Right. We're good." We had agreed to that. It had been the groundwork we laid for our unclassifiable relationship. Under every circumstance, our research came first—always and forever.

"I can see myself out," he said.

I placed the shoes back on the step. "I'll lock up behind you."

"No need. I have my key."

The reminder that he had a key to my house and I had one to his delivered a pang of guilt at my refusal of his offer. "All right. Please be sure to latch the storm door."

He nodded again, lifting a hand in a low wave. "See you Monday, Dr. Carlson."

"Monday, Dr. Cartwright."

I didn't follow him. I waited until I heard the shutting of the door. Once I did, I retraced his steps back to the kitchen and double-checked the lock on the wooden door. He'd locked it from the outside. From the inside there was an extra bolt. With a twist of my wrist it was secure.

LAUREL

*T*he disorientation that met me upon waking sent my mind reeling. When sleep hadn't come last night after Russ left, I took a sleeping pill. It wasn't something I did often. However, as a researcher of pharmaceuticals, I was aware of medications' benefits as well as their drawbacks.

Last night, my mind and body needed rest. To shut off the reel in my head replaying my encounter with the mysterious man, the discussion with Damien, and even Russ's late-night attempt at seduction, I needed assistance.

The result wasn't immediate. I'd tossed and turned until the drug's effects settled my thoughts, allowing me to sleep. However, even in slumber, my thoughts were lost to a world of timeless scenes. Upon disconnecting from reality, my unconsciousness filled with dreams taking on no sequence of time or space.

The air around me was hot and heavy, coating my skin with perspiration despite the constant hum of the air conditioning. The filtered air did little more than circulate the heat and lessen the echoing of explosives in the distance.

I was back in my graduate studies.

Not really.

I was back in an undisclosed location fulfilling a graduate clinical for an independent source. Despite the hardships, selection had been a sought-after position. After a lengthy process, I was accepted. It had been disclosed that if chosen, I would be privy to a highly sensitive assignment. Reams of contracts vowing nondisclosure were presented to me and the other chosen graduate assistants.

Through it all, we were reassured that our assignment was an honor—something to enhance our curriculum vitae. Six weeks in a foreign land completing our duties would result in significant experience that would count toward our clinical requirement. The opportunity was difficult to pass up.

Though we were never given the specifics, the research happening was for a drug—a compound—similar to the one Russ and I were now working on, a memory suppressor. We were told that we were assisting with the clinical trials that had been approved. For security reasons they were being conducted outside of the United States.

Never once were we told our exact location.

At the time, I'd been young, naïve, and enough in awe of the work to accept their explanations.

My duties consisted mostly of crunching numbers and verifying conclusions with endless hours spent documenting refereed-source citations. In other words, I was assigned grunt work. Yet I was part of something bigger, something great.

My role was apart from the real action. There were clinical trials occurring. I saw the data, but not the small subset of participants. The hands-on application took place in an area limited to those people with higher clearance.

In my slumber, I found myself wandering the concrete halls of that facility. *The steel doors closed, their locks echoing as the units were separated. I reached out to the concrete, wishing to absorb the coolness within the cement blocks. Above my head was the ever-present breeze of air conditioning that barely dented the heat hanging in the air.*

An endless maze.

I was lost, wandering beyond my rank, turning corners, and slipping through open doors.

The hallway narrowed with locked doors on each side.

The small reinforced window allowed a glimpse into the room.

It was a participant, lying on a bed. He or she was covered in bandages—a living mummy.

Panic washed through me.

Fear of being caught.

I shouldn't be where I was.

However, curiosity was the key to success.

Why would bandages be needed for a psychotropic drug?

I reached for the doorknob to enter. It was locked.

Why was the participant in a locked room?

My jiggling of the handle must have been audible. The participant's gaze went to the window, peering at me from small openings in the white bandages. Though hidden, the intensity of the stare caused me to stumble backward.

Gasping, I spun away from the window and began to run...

Waking with a start, the scene in my head seemed as real as that world had been that summer nearly seven years ago. Perspiration glued my nightgown to my skin as I threw back the covers and stared upward at the ceiling, allowing my pulse to slow and skin to cool.

Though the dream felt real, it wasn't. That scene hadn't happened.

Actually, the work ceased. One day everything changed.

The research was suddenly halted in its tracks.

After almost four weeks abroad, our six-week assignment ended abruptly—we were called home.

Under the cover of night all of the graduate students were transported via a helicopter to a waiting plane. Within twenty-four hours we were back in the States and given no explanation.

Our promised clinical hours came through, yet our work was left incomplete. And due to the classified nature, the information we learned could not be used in our thesis or cited on our curriculum vitae despite earlier assurances.

Later, I looked through refereed journals and online publications for published results from that research. I figured possibly some of the data could help with our current research.

It was as if my graduate experience was simply a dream.

Even now, any evidence of the trials, the research, or even the facility where we lived and worked was nonexistent.

I hadn't thought of that graduate opportunity in years.

Now upon waking, it was the man without a name who entered my thoughts. There was no possibility he was connected to that scene, but then why did I have that dream?

Did my subconscious know more than my conscious mind?

Maybe if I knew his name, he wouldn't stand out.

As if a name alone could erase his presence and aura, the tenor of his speech, or his calculated control. It wasn't as if a name could lessen the anxiety over his offer—his threat. My stomach twisted as I thought about our research.

I couldn't stop it.

I wouldn't.

Dreams consisted of images from the past as well as ones the mind created. Instead of fact, they were fiction.

Turning on the light, I reached for the black card now on my bedside stand. The man wasn't a dream. He was real.

I'd seen him, felt the heat of his stare, and breathed in the decadence of his cologne.

The only logical explanation I could think of connecting the past with the present was the man's offer, or threat, that could end our research.

All I knew for certain was that the man told me to call

him with a price, a price to sell out my data, a price that didn't exist.

It wasn't that I didn't dream of riches.

Didn't everyone?

It was that those fantasies didn't bring me the sense of satisfaction that came with discoveries. The university paid us well enough for our work. I'd never be rich. I was comfortable. If it was riches I wanted, accepting Sinclair's offer would accomplish that without ending our research.

What we were doing wasn't about money. It was about the potential of helping people, creating an avenue for victims to move beyond traumatic memories. The possibilities were so much more than war-related PTSD. Everyday people suffered from traumatic memories. Many tried to push through, yet the mind wouldn't allow it. We could help...

Victims of car accidents, too afraid to drive.

Victims of abuse, unsure who to ever trust.

Victims of robberies, afraid to shop again.

Truly, the list of traumatic incidents that affected people's lives was endless. All different and yet we were finding the connection. Memories could be triggered by a plethora of stimuli.

The hope was that the compound we'd created would isolate those specific memories, not take them away, and once isolated, inhibit the body's psychological and psychological responses by blocking the brain's ability to release cortisol and norepinephrine along with other neurochemical responses to traumatic memories.

It wasn't our goal to eliminate fear.

Fear was important.

It kept people safe. The uncomfortable feeling that stopped one from entering a dark alley at night or kept someone away from a dangerous ledge was important to maintain.

Irrational fear triggered by memories was our target.

The shrill ring of my phone cut through the otherwise quiet morning air.

Reaching for it, I read the screen.

DR. ERIC OLSEN.

Taking a deep breath, I answered, "Hello, Eric."

"Laurel, I know we were all at the convention center until late last night and this is Saturday..."

"Yes, to all of that," I said, knowing there was more coming.

"Can you meet me at the coffee shop by campus, say at ten o'clock?"

The coffee shop?

"The little one on Tenth Street?" I asked.

"Yes, that's the one. I'll be in a booth."

I looked at the clock. Despite the odd dreams, I'd managed to drift in and out until nearly seven-thirty; nevertheless, a cup of coffee was welcomed. "Yes, I can be there. What is this about?" I couldn't help but wonder if he'd somehow learned about the unusual offer from my mystery man.

"We'll talk about it when you and Russell get here."

I'd hoped for more information, but it sounded like I'd learn more soon. "Okay, Eric. I'll be there."

"See you then."

"Bye."

Eric said Russ would be there too. I knew one other person who might have picked up information or conversations last night. Before getting out of bed, I called my assistant.

"Dr. Carlson?" Stephanie asked, her voice groggy.

"Steph, I'm sorry to bother you so early. I was wondering if you heard any tidbits last night."

"About?"

"Sinclair Pharmaceuticals or maybe that man who stood up to Damien."

"No one mentioned the man. It was kind of strange. I talked to Pam, Dr. Oaks's assistant. She didn't know who he was either. It was like he just showed up."

"He said he would make an offer. Have any anonymous offers been made? He said for the sole right. It would have to be a big offer."

"I can try to find out. I'm sorry. I was exhausted last night and once it was over, I came home and crashed."

I nodded my head, though she couldn't see me. "I get that. If you learn anything, please let me know. But..."

"What?" she asked.

"I don't know. I have a weird feeling. Try to find out without being too obvious. The whole Sinclair element..." I didn't add the part about the man. "...has me uncomfortable."

"I'll be as stealthy as possible."

"Thanks, Steph. Sorry for waking you."

"I was planning to get up in the next hour or two anyway."

That made me smile. "See you Monday, but if you learn anything..."

"I'll let you know as soon as I do."

"Thanks, bye."

LAUREL

Sherrill's Coffee Shoppe had been a staple near the university since long before I took my position. The mom-and-pop feel and delicious pastries added to its fame. It was no secret that every morning Eric stopped on his way to the university and picked up his large cup of caffeinated fuel.

The parking was limited because originally this location was mostly for students who lived on campus and could walk. The campus had grown so much that now most students were commuters. Luckily there was a space for my car a few businesses down on the street. As I parked, I scanned the area, searching for Russ's black Chevy truck. It was usually easy to spot. I'd teased him that if I didn't know him as well as I did, I would have said he was overcompensating.

The truck was decked out with every bell and whistle.

And knowing him as well as I did, he might be—a little.

Opening the door to Sherrill's, the aroma of fresh donuts, cakes, and of course, coffee, infused my bloodstream with a jolt of caffeine and sugar, all without consuming a thing. I'd planned to order at the counter first, but as soon as I spotted Dr. Olsen, I changed my mind, going first to him.

His expression was one of a man on the brink of something. I just wasn't sure what.

"Eric, are you all right?"

"Laurel, have a seat," he said, gesturing to the other side of the booth. "I wanted to discuss something with you that came to my attention."

"Should we wait for Russ?" I asked, laying my coat next to me on the vinyl seat.

"I asked him to be here at 10:15."

There was something in his voice that set my nerves on alert. "I'm not sure what you heard..." I nibbled on my lip as I debated if I should talk to him about the odd encounter last night, and then I decided to go another route. "...is it about Russ?"

Eric closed his eyes as he ran his hand over his face. It was then that I noticed his unshaved cheeks and unkempt appearance. In all the years I'd been in this department, I couldn't recall seeing him less than impeccable. Even at parties or cookouts with other faculty, he was casual but put together.

"After the gathering last night," he began, "I was summoned to Dr. Oaks's office."

"To his office?"

If he was summoned to the dean's office, that meant after Eric left the convention center, he drove back to the university. It wasn't a far distance, yet it seemed impractical after the long night.

"You can imagine my surprise when Damien Sinclair was also present."

At the sound of Damien's name, my stomach dropped and neck straightened. "What happened?"

"The early numbers were promising from our attendees. Now...I'm not sure if any of that matters."

"Why did you want to talk to me first?" I asked.

"Damien announced to both of us that Russell has verbally agreed to take the research to Sinclair. He also said that Russell promised he'd make an effort to convince you to do the same."

My head was shaking. "No. The university deserves credit. If we sell out to Sinclair, we'll lose any chance to be involved in determining the on-label use. Besides, there's more research that needs to be done." My mind was jumbled. "They'll be thinking dollar signs and trying to rush everything."

Eric inhaled, leaned back against the tall seat, and exhaled. "Have you spoken to Russell since the event?"

"Yes," I said, my voice quieter than before.

"He called you?"

"He showed up at my house last night."

Eric didn't respond verbally; however, by the way his neck

stiffened, he wasn't pleased. We hadn't broadcast our private connections and I didn't plan to do that now.

"He came by, saying he was worried about me." I tried to recall the conversation. "I don't remember it all. I was exhausted."

"Did he mention Damien or Sinclair Pharmaceuticals?"

My head shook as I tried to recall all that we'd talked about. "He did, but not like you're saying, not like Damien said. No, I remember. Russ said Damien made him an offer—no particulars—and Russ told him to stick it up his ass."

"He didn't try to convince you to join him at Sinclair?"

"The opposite. We discussed how we didn't want to leave the university." I shrugged. "We didn't talk that long."

"Oh?"

"I told him to leave. As I said, I was tired."

Eric looked down as he wrapped his hands around his cup of coffee. "I need to know where you stand." Though his face was still down toward his coffee, his eyes peered upward to me. "Maybe we shouldn't tell Russell what Damien said?"

"No."

"No?"

I sat taller. "Russ and I have worked on this together. I'm not going to lie to him now."

"It's not lying, Laurel. It's keeping our cards hidden until more are revealed."

"I don't like it," I said as I began to scoot from the booth. "I'm going to get a cup of coffee." I nodded toward his cup. "Can I get anything for you?"

As I stood, Eric's gaze went beyond me, his eyes set. Turning, I caught Russell's entrance and then shifting back to Eric, I said, "I'll let you two talk for a minute."

"Laurel..."

Russell came toward me. "Looks like I'm the last to the party."

I tilted my head toward the booth. "I haven't been here long. I'm just now getting coffee. Do you want anything?"

He reached for my hand and lowered his voice. "After he's done with us, I owe you an apology for last night."

I shook my head. "No apologies. Coffee?"

His lips quirked upward. "You know how I take it."

"I do."

Walking to the counter, my thoughts went to everything Eric had said. Part of me doubted that he'd shared the whole story. There was more to this if it prompted him to lose sleep and meet with us unshaven. I stood behind two young women, probably students, I thought, as I waited and eyed the pastries behind the glass.

When it was my turn, I told the lady behind the counter my order.

As I reached for my purse, the air previously filled with scents of coffees and sugars shifted with the infusion of birch and black-currant spices. Gasping at the recognized scent, I stood taller as the lady looked past me. Afraid to turn, I peered down at my own feet. Directly behind me all I could see were the toes of black cowboy boots—large boots. Heat flooded through me as if a furnace's register had opened behind me.

"Ma'am, that will be four dollars and fifteen cents." Though she was talking to me, her eyes fluttered about as if she couldn't hold my stare.

A large hand came from behind me, a five-dollar bill in its grasp.

His deep voice shattered the din of the crowd. "I'll take care of the lady's order."

Though I tried to turn as the lady took his cash, his other hand on my waist prevented me from facing him. Warm breath grazed my neck as he lowered his mouth to my ear.

"Don't do it. Don't say anything."

My skin prickled as I searched for assistance. There was none. The lady who'd taken the cash was now busy with my order. "I haven't," I replied.

"I know that." His deep whisper rumbled through me. "I know everything. I know more than you about what is happening."

"I don't under—"

"I gave you a week, but for your own good, I suggest you get that price sooner rather than later. Things are moving quicker than I predicted."

The lady returned with two cups of coffee. "Here you go," she said, her smile fading. "Who was that?"

I spun, knowing that the heat from a moment ago was gone. Turning back, I shook my head. "No idea."

Taking the cups, I walked away from the counter as she

helped the next customer. My gaze scanned the entire shop. Most tables were occupied and there were people entering, but no sight of the man. It was as if he hadn't been there.

Except he had. The lady behind the counter saw him.

With my thoughts all over the place, I set the coffee on the table as Russ scooted deeper into the booth.

"Thanks," he said, reaching for his cup. When his eyes met mine, he asked, "Are you all right?"

I came to rest beside Russ. "I-I'm...there's just a lot happening."

Eric sat taller. "What you two have done...what you've accomplished...it's more than I imagined. It's more involved and bigger than anything our university has ever seen. As you can imagine, Dr. Oaks is concerned with the ongoing costs."

"But the potential..." I said, worried that would never be learned.

"It will make money," Russ said. "Sinclair knows that. That's why they want it."

"What do you want?" Eric asked.

I turned to Russ as our eyes met again. "I want..." I looked to Eric. "...to finish our research."

"Russell?" Eric asked.

"Yeah, me too."

"Where?"

"Not at Sinclair," I volunteered.

When I looked at Russ, he nodded.

LAUREL

"*H*ello?" Despite my attempt to sound awake, my voice cracked with the grogginess of sleep.

With everything going on, the ringing of my phone had my mind on full alert. It had been four days since the gathering, and while my mystery man hadn't reappeared, it seemed that my time was running out.

"Hello," I said again.

Who was calling me in the middle of the night?

Was it the man wanting an answer?

I was no closer to being able to answer him. I didn't have a price.

My eyes squinted, bringing the red numerals of the clock on my bedside stand into focus: 3:19.

"Hello," I repeated again, pulling the phone away from my ear and looking at the number on the screen. BLOCKED. I sucked in a breath, about ready to hang up. It was common knowledge that nothing good came from calls in the middle of the night.

Why had I answered it?

I knew the answer. I hadn't looked, but now that I had, I hoped.

Please be the man telling me it was all a joke.

If it were him, maybe he could provide me with some more information. Since the night of the gathering, Dr. Olsen was still acting oddly, Russ seemed preoccupied, and Stephanie hadn't learned more about the uninvited guest or of any anonymous offers of funding. The two variables I hadn't had contact with were the mysterious man and Damien Sinclair.

Pushing myself upward, I sat against the headboard, my hand gripping the phone tighter as I counted in my head. 'Five, four, three...' I wasn't going to just sit here in silence. 'Two...'

Forget this.

As disappointment washed over me, I reached for the red button on the screen, the one that would allow me to disconnect the line. This person had one more second.

'One—'

Before I could disconnect the call, a voice came through the phone.

"Dr. Carlson."

From the two simple words I deduced that the speaker

was a man—but not the man I'd hoped to hear. It wasn't a voice I recognized.

While this man's address hadn't been stated as a question, whoever this was expected an answer. "Yes, this is Dr. Carlson speaking."

"Doctor, I'm Detective Lanky. I'm sorry to have bothered you at this hour; however, there's been a situation. As we speak, we have two plainclothes officers on their way to your home. Please be ready to leave with them as soon as they arrive."

My head shook. "Wait. What? What situation?"

"It's your lab at the university, Doctor. There's been a break-in. I don't want to frighten you; however, due to what happened, we're taking every precaution."

"I don't understand."

"Doctor, there are two things. First, we'd like your assistance to determine what, if anything, is missing or destroyed. It is also believed that you could be in danger. After we complete the inventory, you'll be taken to a secure location."

"Secure? Danger? M-my lab?" My mind swirled a thousand different directions, cyclical like a cyclone spinning faster and faster.

Stolen?

Destroyed?

"Destroyed? What do you mean?" Somehow in my head, the fate of our lab and our work superseded his other warnings.

No longer sleepy, my eyes had adjusted to the faint light in my room from the moonlight seeping around the blinds. I took in the empty bed beside me, reaching out and running the palm of my hand over the cool sheets as a pang of concern washed through me.

"What about Dr. Cartwright?" I asked into the phone. "He'd stayed later than I at the lab last night and my assistant, Stephanie Moore. She was still there when I left. Was anyone hurt?"

I recalled saying good night to Stephanie and Russ. I'd asked Russ if he wanted to share a dinner. I was still feeling guilty about the way I turned him down the other night. He'd smiled, saying he wasn't ready to leave the office and that he had data to review.

A rain check.

That was what he'd said.

"Dr. Cartwright and Ms. Moore?" I repeated

"Doctor," Detective Lanky replied, lowering his voice, "please listen carefully. Your safety is our priority. The officers should be at your home in approximately ten minutes. This is very important. Do not answer the door to anyone else. Do not answer or make any other calls."

What had once been a cyclone of thoughts zeroed in on the obvious: Detective Lanky hadn't answered my question about Russ or Stephanie. Our lab and offices, in what was labeled a secure research facility, had been breached, and he'd said that I could be in danger.

"What about Dr. Olsen?" I asked, doing my best to think straight.

"Dr. Carlson, for your own safety, please follow my directions."

My safety.

Their safety.

The same words were being repeated.

"Umm. Okay."

Something felt off, wrong.

Shouldn't speaking to a member of some form of law enforcement make me feel safer?

It wasn't.

"I'm sorry, Detective, please tell me again which law enforcement agency you represent."

"Ma'am, as I said, the officers arriving will be plainclothes officers. They'll have identification. After you make an assessment of the facility, we will get you to a safe location."

"I-I..."

We had protocol for emergencies.

This wasn't it.

"Doctor, can we count on you?"

Instead of answering right away, I flung back the covers and looked down at my sleeping attire. Boy shorts and a camisole were hardly the clothes I wanted to wear to survey our lab and offices. "I-I need to get dressed before they arrive."

"Dr. Carlson, we're very sorry. We'll do the best we can to keep you safe."

Sorry?

"I-I'll be ready."

"Thank you, Dr. Carlson."

"Detective—"

The phone call ended before I could find out why he was sorry and why I was in danger.

Russ.

I didn't care what Detective Lanky said, if I was in danger and it was in relation to a break-in at our lab, then Russ would be also. Waiting until my screen darkened, I swiped it, bringing it back to life. With one touch I hit the icon for calls and touched Russ's name.

My heart thumped in my chest as the call rang.

Once.

Twice.

"Hello. You have reached—"

Shit!

Disconnecting the call, I spoke aloud, "Russ, where are you? Please be okay."

Next, continuing to ignore the detective's warning, I tried Eric Olsen's number. His number rang three times before his voice mail picked up.

The wind rattled my windows while farther away, Mrs. Beeson's gate banged against the latch. "It's just the spring wind," I said, speaking to myself as I turned on the light by the bed and scanned all four corners of my bedroom. The room was exactly as it had been before I fell asleep, exactly as it had been the day before and the day before that.

I was nothing if not consistent.

One more call. I hit Stephanie's name. Another voice mail.

The rooms within my century-old home were small with wood floors, wood trim, and high ceilings. Upon the outside wall between two tall windows was a stone wood-burning fireplace. It was directly above the one in the living room on the first floor. Though I never used the one in the bedroom, the way the chimney whistled added to the noises that now seemed more pronounced.

Perhaps the only difference within my bedroom was the outfit strewn over the chair in the corner. Each night the day's clothes ended up there until morning when they went in with the dirty clothes, and the chair waited for the next day's outfit.

I laid my phone on the bedside stand.

Nibbling on my lower lip, I zeroed my gaze on the doorway leading to the hallway. I hadn't closed my bedroom door completely last night, leaving it slightly ajar. It wasn't like I needed privacy. I lived alone.

Now, however, the dark hallway combined with the call gave me an ominous feeling.

"Stop it, Laurel. The police—or whoever they are—will be here soon." I took a deep breath and stood.

The black card came to mind.

Why would I call it now?

What would I say?

Would I ask if he'd been the one to break into my lab?

That was ridiculous.

Squaring my shoulders, I made my way to the attached bathroom. An owner of the house prior to me added a pocket door connecting the bathroom to the master bedroom, creating an en-suite bath, something unheard of at the time this house was originally constructed.

As I hit another switch, the bathroom filled with light. Pulling my dark hair back into a low ponytail, I splashed a bit of cool water on my face and looked into my eyes. Red lines webbed the white around the blue. I hadn't had a decent night's sleep since that gathering. It wasn't only my eyes. There were dark circles beneath them and pallor in my cheeks.

Too bad.

This wasn't a makeup occasion.

It was the middle of the night, and I needed to be ready when the officers came to get me.

As I took care of business, my mind filled with more questions.

Could this be connected to the no-name mystery man?

Or was it connected to Damien Sinclair?

What about Russ, Stephanie, and Eric? Were they safe?

The more I thought, the more I questioned. Taking a deep breath as I washed my hands, I reached for a towel. My mind was doing a mental inventory, thinking about what could be stolen—or what could have been the target.

It seemed obvious.

Our research.

It was classified.

Prior to last Friday, I would have said that few other people knew about what we were doing. Now I knew that wasn't the case.

Could the culprit be someone who was in attendance Friday night?

It didn't make sense that anyone would or could breach the security around the facility, yet if they did, they wouldn't find what they wanted. That was why Russ and I divided the results every night, each taking our part. Of course, there was information secured on the lab computers, but not all of the critical components.

Where had I put my flash drive?

I rushed back into the bedroom and tossed yesterday's blouse from the chair. Picking up the slacks, I reached into the pockets.

There it was.

The simple flash drive that held a wealth of information.

Usually when I got home, I hid it inside the fireplace within my room. There was a loose stone. I figured it was protected there. However, last night I'd been too consumed with other thoughts.

I jumped as the ring of my phone filled the air. Walking to the bedside I read the screen: STEPHANIE.

"Oh, thank God," I whispered as I hit the green icon. "Steph, you're all right?"

"I-I guess. I didn't answer your call because I'd just finished with another one."

My heart beat faster at the sound of her apprehension. "From whom?"

"He said he was a police detective and something happened at the university. Dr. Carlson, they told me not to call anyone, but you called me. So...do you know what's happening?"

"I don't." I looked down at the flash drive in my other hand. "I got the same call. Two officers are coming to get me."

"They said the same thing to me. I'm scared," Stephanie confessed.

"Me too. I'm glad you're all right. I can't reach Russ."

"He was still in his office when I left. You don't think..."

"Did the caller say they're taking you to the university, the police officers?" I asked.

"They said they wanted me to see if anything was missing from my office."

"Okay, we're going to the same place. I'll see you there."

"This isn't the protocol Dr. Olsen put in place."

She was right. This change had my stomach in knots. "We'll be there together. I need to hang up."

"See you soon," she said before the call ended.

Hurriedly, I stepped into a pair of jeans, stuck the flash drive in the pocket, and pulled a sweatshirt over my head. After donning a pair of socks, I was tying my shoes when a familiar sound sent a new chill running down my spine. The small hairs on the back of my neck jumped to life.

"Old houses make noise. It's probably the wind," I whispered to myself.

It could have been the wind, but it wasn't the whistle of the chimney or the bang of Mrs. Beeson's gate. I knew those sounds.

It had been the slap of my storm door hitting against the house.

There had been one hit.

I stood perfectly still and waited. If it had been the wind, which I told myself it was, the slam should recur. It always did.

Silence.

The red numerals on the clock changed. It had been five minutes since I hung up with Detective Lanky. The officers wouldn't be at my side door. They wouldn't open it without knocking.

Right?

Law-abiding police officers wouldn't. Besides, law enforcement couldn't just enter a private residence without a warrant. Years of television crime shows taught me that. There was an exception—if someone was in danger.

My pulse raced as I turned again toward the partially open door to my room.

Before I could convince myself that I was safe, another sound confirmed my fear.

This wasn't my imagination.

The palms of my hands grew clammy.

Old houses have their unique quirks. The fourth step of the staircase to the second level also needed repair. My dad mentioned that instead of nails, the builders should have used screws.

My knees grew weak as I heard the distinctive groan of the wood pulling on the nails.

My gaze darted about my bedroom. I could run for the door to the hallway, slam it closed, and turn the old lock. As I willed my feet to move, I remembered the small canister of pepper spray in my bedside stand.

My tennis shoes squeaked on the shiny wood floor as I hurried to the nightstand and opened the top drawer. Staring up at me from the surface was the black card. Quickly, I pushed that into my pocket. And then, my hands no longer trembling but nearly convulsing, I reached for the small pouch within the drawer.

The door behind me opened wider with a creak as an overwhelming sense of dread washed through me. Dizziness came on as my blood rushed to my feet. The onset of fear was overwhelming, rendering my body useless as if paralyzed.

I was afraid to turn, to meet whoever was here.

His voice reverberated through the air, ricocheting off the walls. And then I knew.

"Laurel, we need to get out of here."

LAUREL

*S*pinning around, I clutched the canister to my chest. "Shit, Russ, you almost got a face full of pepper spray." And then, before I could process, I stepped toward him, wrapped my arms around his neck, and let my forehead drop to his shoulder. My entire body trembled, the mix of emotions creating a concoction that flooded my bloodstream as fear gave way to relief. "Thank God. You're okay."

After a moment, his arms surrounded my waist. "You are, too. I was worried."

Taking a step back I looked up into his eyes. "What the hell is happening? How did you get here so fast after the call?"

"What call?" Russ shook his head as he reached for the canister of pepper spray, removed it from my shaky grasp, and tossed it onto the bed. "I should have told you..." His words trailed away. "...everything."

"Tell me what? Is this about our research?"

His head began turning as his eyes searched the bedroom. "Listen, I changed my mind and that's why I'm here. Grab your stuff. We don't have time to explain." He reached for my hand. "Do you trust me, Laurel?"

"Changed your mind...about what?" I asked.

"Do you trust me?" he repeated his question.

I nodded. I did trust him.

"Then listen. We need to get out of here. Once we get away from this mess, I'll explain everything, I promise." He turned back to me, scanning my clothes. "Why weren't you asleep?"

"I told you. I was awakened by a call; some detective said that someone broke into our lab. I asked about you. He didn't answer me." A debilitating wave of emotion washed through me, knotting my stomach and weakening my knees.

I collapsed on the edge of the bed with a sigh as my eyes stayed fixed on Russ. "I was so worried that you were there when someone..."

Russ knelt to his haunches at my feet and laid his hand on my knee. "Stay strong. We're almost there. What else did they say? Did they mention Eric?"

My eyes widened as I shook my head. "What about Eric?"

"Come on," he said, standing and pulling me to my feet. "I'll tell you everything I know once we're out of here."

"Did something happen to him?" My mind was immediately filled with images of Dr. Eric Olsen. He'd interviewed me for my position at the university. He'd been my friend and my mentor. "Tell me," I insisted.

"Fuck," Russ said with an exasperated breath. "This wasn't supposed to happen like this—none of it." His expression pleaded as he again reached for my hands and surrounded them with his grasp. Holding them tightly, he brought them to his chest. "You've got to believe me, Laurel. It wouldn't have happened. If only Dr. Oaks wasn't so fucking greedy. That gathering was a mistake and ever since, the shit has been hitting the fan."

He was right about that.

"Dr. Oaks, greedy?" I asked. "What are you talking about?" My mind continued to spin images of the gathering in my head. "Is this about Damien or someone else?"

Letting go of my hands, Russ took a step back, his expression hardening. "I came to get you. To help you."

"What are you talking about?" When he didn't answer, I went on, "Russ, did someone find your price?"

"I told you. There's no price I'd put on our research."

"That man at the gathering, the one who put Damien in his place, who was he?"

Russ's palm lightly came to my cheek. "I'll tell you everything I know and you can do the same. We just can't do it here." His head shook. "We need to find someplace safe. Fuck knows that doesn't include the lab either."

"Where will we go?"

"I don't know. We'll figure it out."

"The police are coming. They can help," I reasoned aloud.

"What?"

"I told you. The phone call was from a detective. He said two plainclothes officers were on their way to get me. They want an evaluation of what's missing, if anything is."

"Shit." His eyes widened. "Turn off the lights."

"Why?"

Russ rushed past me, turning off the lamp beside my bed and hurrying to the switch in the bathroom, leaving us with only the moonlight from around the blinds.

"Russ, this is scaring me."

"Good. We have to get out of here before they arrive. Get your coat. I'll explain it all once we're in my truck."

"My coat's downstairs."

"Then come on." He again reached for my hand.

Keeping my feet from moving, I tugged back. "The man on the phone said he was a detective. He never told me from what department. Are you saying he probably wasn't a police officer or some kind of law enforcement?"

"I don't know. I just know that we don't have time to talk." Russ gave my hand a yank, pulling me toward the darkened hallway and staircase.

When we reached the bottom of the stairs, the blue LED shine of headlights floated across the otherwise dark living room.

"What if that's them?" I asked.

"Did that car just pull into your driveway?" Russ's voice was low.

"I think so." The blood again drained from my extremities, leaving me light-headed. Maintaining a whisper, I said, "We can't get out. Even if they go to the front door, they'll see us if we leave through the side door."

"The French doors," he said, continuing to tug me toward the back of the house to the doors that led to a small stone patio.

I pulled my coat from the back of a kitchen chair and grabbed my purse as Russ twisted the lock on the old door. The knob turned in his hand, yet the door didn't budge.

"Pull. They stick," I said softly, reminding him how the years of paint and moisture made the doors difficult to open.

Doing as I said, he pulled. After a pop, one of the doors opened inward. At the same time, the front door's doorbell chimed, echoing throughout the house. I looked toward the living room. From our perspective we were hidden from view from the front door. We couldn't see who was ringing the bell and they couldn't see us.

"Shit, we should have grabbed—"

Interrupting, I reached for his hand. "Russ, what's happening?"

Instead of answering, he nodded at my purse. "Do you have your flash drive?"

"Yes."

"Then we don't need the other. Let's go."

"Dr. Carlson, Indianapolis Metro Police." The voice came through the front door.

I stopped in my tracks. "Russ?"

"Fuck. We'll tell them I spent the night."

"Then why would I have asked about you?"

"You were tired, delirious."

I shook my head. "What are you trying to hide?"

The doorbell chimed again.

Russ reached for my hand after he closed the French door. "I don't know who is out there. All I know is that we can't tell anyone about Sinclair's offer."

"Why?"

"Because Sinclair threatened Eric." His words were rushed. "Damien thinks it's Eric who is standing in the way of us going to them."

I gasped. "Threatened him? In the way of...what? I don't understand. And I don't want to go to Sinclair. It's my decision, not based on Eric."

"If we say anything, it could jeopardize more than his life. We have to play dumb."

As the doorbell rang again, I took a deep breath and turned, walking toward the door. With a flip of a switch, I turned on the porch light. One man came into view. Wearing a dark suit with an unbuttoned overcoat, the officer stood taller than me as I pulled the wooden door inward. Though the glass door was between us, a breeze blew against my skin.

"Dr. Carlson," the man said.

I tried to steady my voice. "Detective Lanky said you'd have identification?"

"Of course." The man reached into his overcoat and removed a wallet. He flipped it open, showing me his Indianapolis Metro Police Department identification complete with his picture and badge.

I read his name: Officer Peter Stanley.

I had no idea if the identification was real. It looked real and so did his badge.

"Doctor, may I come in?" Officer Stanley asked.

My first instinct was to comply, and then I remembered what I'd seen on television. "Do you have a search warrant?"

As I asked, a voice came from the way of the kitchen. "Dr. Carlson?"

With the glass storm door still closed, I spun and took a step to the side, clearing the view into the kitchen. Although I expected to see Russell, I didn't. Instead, there was a man I didn't recognize standing in the open archway of my French doors.

"Doctor, why were these doors open?" the man asked.

"Dr. Carlson, that is Officer Manes," Officer Stanley volunteered.

"Fine, yes," I said to Officer Stanley, "you may come in." I unlatched the storm door and after motioning for him to enter, I turned and walked back into the kitchen, my gaze darting about.

Where was Russ?

My coat was on the table where I'd dropped it, next to my purse that was no longer latched.

"Doctor?" Officer Manes said with a questioning inflection to his voice.

I pulled my gaze away from my purse and shook my head. "I don't know. It was closed."

"Ma'am, I can't open your door without a warrant. They were opened wide when I stepped into your backyard."

I waved Officer Manes into the house. "You may join us."

My attention went back to my purse. Picking it up, I peered inside, doing a quick inventory. As best I could tell, it seemed like everything was present and accounted for.

The presence of these two men was overwhelming in my small kitchen. Even with the recent renovations, I didn't have the luxury of a walk-in pantry or even a broom closet. There were no other options for Russ's whereabouts. It had to be that he'd opened the back doors when he'd left.

"Would you like me to close these?" Officer Manes asked, reaching for the French doors.

"Please."

"Doctor, as Detective Lanky mentioned, we would like your assistance surveying your lab and office. The alarm wasn't triggered. A custodian came upon the aftermath. We believe this has to do with your research."

I shook my head. "How does the police department know about a research project at the university?"

"It's our job to know," Officer Manes said, turning again toward the doors and my back patio. "Was anyone else here?"

Were there footprints?

Did he know?

"My neighbor...her gate unlatches and bangs in the wind. I

went over there earlier in the evening to secure it. I must not have latched the doors properly."

His expression gave no indication of whether or not he believed my half-truth. The true part was that I had secured Mrs. Beeson's gate yesterday. It was in the early evening and I'd used my side door. Nevertheless, the information was basically accurate.

"Doctor, are you ready to go with us?"

More knots formed in my stomach, auxiliary knots on top of others.

Why had Russell left me?

What could I say?

Was Eric really in danger?

Was I?

I nodded as I reached for the coat I'd dropped to the kitchen table. "Yes. Let's get this over with."

Officer Manes shook his head. "The task force recommends taking you somewhere safe until we learn more about the break-in. Do you have a bag packed?"

"What? No. Detective Lanky said..." I tried to recall. Too much had happened. "...I need to assure my family and friends."

"One thing at a time," Officer Stanley said. "Doctor, we can wait. Please hurry and pack a bag with enough items to last a few days."

"I'll be a minute," I said, walking out of the kitchen to the stairs.

I didn't even think to turn on a light as I ascended the

stairs. It was my home, and there were two police officers in the kitchen. It wasn't until I entered my bedroom that I felt a presence.

"Russ—?"

The bedroom door closed as my scream began to form. The process had begun—the inhalation of air and the opening of my mouth. It was primed and ready, and yet the shriek didn't leave my throat. Everything was blocked as a large hand came over my mouth and an arm around my waist. The entirety of my body was jerked backward, pulling me to my toes until my back collided with a solid chest.

"Don't scream."

LAUREL

"Tell me you won't scream," the deep voice reverberated, his whisper intensified by the proximity of our bodies. Mine was once again trembling, caused by more than hearing his words—I felt his demand all the way to my core.

"Tell me."

Unable to respond verbally, I nodded, moving my head as best I could.

"I won't hurt you." His warm breath skirting across my exposed neck offered me reassurance while the rigidity of his body sent another message.

His grip of me, the way he held me against him, offered no softness or comfort. Though I couldn't see his face, I knew without a doubt that this was the man from the gathering. I didn't know how he'd entered my house or how long he'd been present. At the moment, that seemed irrelevant. All that mattered was he was here now.

His cologne from before was replaced by a masculine scent reminding me of outdoors. This man was wind and rain and cool spring nights with the fury and power notorious with our storms. In his hold, the air around me shifted as if a barometer were falling and the atmosphere was changing.

Slowly, his fingers moved, loosening their grip on my lips.

"How——?" I began.

His hand resumed its position, pressing my lips harder than before, causing them to flatten against my teeth. Though he'd promised otherwise, the pressure brought a copper taste to my tongue and tears to my eyes.

"Don't speak unless you whisper," his command came through gritted teeth. "I'll explain later. Nod if you agree."

Again, I nodded.

Immediately, the pressure lessened. Once his hand was gone from my mouth, I moved my lips and jaw from side to side. Though he'd released my face, I wasn't free. My body was captive to the strength of his grasp. One of his arms was still around my waist holding me tightly against the hardness of him. When he'd released my mouth, he'd moved his other arm across my upper chest, keeping my shoulders to his front.

It was the arm holding my waist that garnered my attention. Though his gruff voice was all business, his body was reacting to our proximity, growing harder against the small of my back.

Fear bubbled with something else in the pit of my

stomach as I fought the urge to turn and see what I could only feel.

"What are you going to do?" I asked, my voice shaky as my body trembled and mind reeled.

His grip tightened, pulling me against him. "I'm here to help you be safe."

"From...?"

"Laurel, you're surrounded by more danger than you realize."

Was the danger downstairs or up here?

He didn't let me respond. Instead, he went on, "Those men downstairs...I haven't had a chance to confirm their identities. Did you see any identification?"

Again, I nodded.

"Did it look real?"

How did he expect me to carry on a conversation like this?

"Did it?"

"I don't know," I whispered, answering honestly.

"Do you recall their badge numbers?"

"No. I saw their names—well, one of them." It was the first time that I realized I hadn't asked for the second officer's identification. "The one I saw, his name was Peter Stanley. The other one was introduced as Officer Manes."

His chest inflated as he took a breath. "I can get you out of here, but it's possible they'll have to die."

"What?"

"If they're who they say they are—IMPD—killing them

will add a whole new level of deception to this mess you're in."

Shouldn't I be petrified hearing a man calmly discuss the murder of police officers?

Shouldn't this conversation have me on the verge of tears?

And yet somehow within his grasp, as my mind and body wrestled with what was right and what was wrong, there was reassurance. With this stranger near me, I could handle whatever happened.

I closed my eyes and continued to listen. When he stopped speaking, I replied, "I don't want anyone to be killed because of me."

"If it's them or you, there's no choice."

"I don't understand. Why..." My head fell forward and body went lax as my words trailed away. There were too many questions to complete that sentence.

"I'm going to let go of you." His words shouldn't cause disappointment, yet for some unknown reason, being in his grip—in his arms—was the securest I'd felt in days. "Can you stand?"

I took a deep breath. "Yes."

His arms began to loosen their hold.

"Keep the light off."

I nodded as his strong arms disappeared, leaving me momentarily void. It was more than his hold; when his arms let go, the warmth of his body vanished along with the sensation of my softness contrasting with his hardness.

"May I turn?" When he didn't respond, I did what I'd

asked, turning to face the stone-hard chest I'd only felt. I lifted my chin. As in the banquet hall with only the two of us, I saw him in the dim lighting. Shadows made his expression more menacing than it had been in the light of the crowded gathering. "Who are you?"

"I'm the man who's going to ensure you live to see the rest of today."

"What if they're really IMPD?"

"Then you should be fine."

"Should be?"

"There's a lot at stake right now and too many players. The list is growing by the second. I haven't figured it all out. I thought I had more time."

My head shook, unsure what this meant. "They said they're IMPD."

"What if they lied?" he asked.

"Do you know about Russ or Eric? Are they safe?"

"I make it my job to know as much as I can about everyone involved in a job."

"Am I your job?" I asked.

"You're part of it. As I told you, my employer wants to stop your research."

"Dr. Carlson?" a male voice called from the floor below.

"Tell them you're coming," the man whispered.

"What are you going to do?"

"Tell them now before they come up here. If they do, I won't have a choice."

I reached for the door handle and opened my bedroom

door. "I'm sorry," I called. "I'm working as fast as I can. I'll be down in just a few more minutes."

After I closed the door, I turned back. "I can't pack without light."

Within the dimness of the room, I saw the man nod. Walking to my bedside stand, I reached for the light and twisted the knob. In the new illumination, my gaze went to the pepper spray on the bed.

"Don't think about it."

I looked up, taking in his hardened expression and the massiveness of his body. This man gave off a presence that made the police officers downstairs seem more like boys than men. I'd been right in my earlier assessment. This man was a storm on the verge of something bigger. Force emanated from him, yet he was immune to the laws of physics.

The law of conservation of energy stated that total energy of an isolated system remained constant—neither created nor destroyed. That didn't apply to the man before me. In his expression I saw that he held the reins, being capable of taming the power of his inner storm or allowing it to strengthen.

There was something intensely striking about him. Not feminine but beautiful in an almost tragic sense of the word. As I recalled the tattooed wrists I'd seen when his cuffs moved at the gathering, I longed to see more of his body.

I pulled my gaze from his green eyes and scanned him from the floor up. On his feet, he wore dark boots that should have made noise, and yet I hadn't heard him. Blue jeans covered his long legs, resting on his hips. They were too loose to accent the hardness I'd felt in the small of my back. I pulled my gaze higher where under an unzipped black jacket, he wore a black thermal, its material stretched across the chest of stone where I'd been held. A vein protruded in his thick neck.

No longer smooth as it had been at the gathering, there was a day or two of beard growth on his set jawline. His hair was pulled back at the nape of his neck. Below his high cheekbones his cheeks were hollowed by the strain of his clenched jaw. Yet through it all, it was the force of his green-eyed stare that sent chills through my nervous system, as if his scanning gaze could set my skin ablaze.

Without a word, he was doing to me as I'd done to him.

I felt each inch of his stare as it moved up my body. Like lasers they moved over me, seeing me, as if my clothes didn't exist.

"Take off your shirt," he demanded.

"What?"

He reached into the pocket of his coat and pulled out a small device. "I can insert this into your bra, and I'll be able to keep track of where they take you and listen to what you and anyone within a few feet say. It also monitors your heart rate. I'll be out of sight, but I will be close if anything happens."

"What if I say no?"

"I inject you with a tranquilizer and get you out of here."

Shit.

If he were monitoring my heart rate right now, I was certain it would be through the roof.

"What does that option mean for those men downstairs?"

"We better hope they aren't IMPD."

"Dr. Carlson? We must hurry." Again the voice came from below.

I walked back to the door and pulled it open. "Almost ready."

The door closed with a thud.

When I turned back around, the man was looking directly at me, the device in the palm of his large hand. Biting my lip, I contemplated my next move. "I-I'm not wearing a bra. I dressed in a hurry."

He tilted his head toward my dresser. "Get one. I'll insert the device while you throw some things in a bag. Or..."

He didn't need to finish the sentence. I would do as he said or he would tranquilize me and kill the men downstairs.

Opening the drawer to my bras, I debated. "Does it matter about the bra?"

"An underwire hides the signal best."

Nodding I pulled out a new white bra I'd recently purchased and handed it to the man—a man I didn't know. "How can I trust you?"

"How can you not?" His fingers ran over the bottom of the cups. "I could have guessed you wore white."

"What does that mean?"

His lips quirked, the first show of emotion I'd seen. "Get some things packed."

As I pulled a small overnight case from my closet, the man sat on the edge of my bed and worked the wire of his device into the bottom of one C cup of my bra. It was as I threw some cosmetics into a plastic bag and shoved them into the suitcase that he stood.

"Now, take off your shirt."

"I could go into the bathroom and put it on?" I hadn't meant it as a question, yet with the inflection of my tone, that was how it sounded.

"No."

Biting my lip, I turned away and lifted the hem of my sweatshirt over my head revealing the camisole I'd worn to bed. Tossing the sweatshirt toward the bed, I took a deep breath and peeled off the layer of satin. The cool air hardened my nipples as goose bumps peppered my skin.

"Laurel, turn around. I need to be sure this is positioned correctly."

"I-I could just..."

His warm hand landed on my bare shoulder. His touch was different than before. "If I was going to take advantage of you, I would have done it by now."

I wasn't sure what to say or do.

"I would have done it," he said, his voice deep and husky, "the night of the gathering. The night I walked in that room and you were there by yourself, so trusting of the world around you. That black dress..." His hand moved over my shoulder. "...your hair..."

"I-I..."

"I could have taken you that night, against the wall or over one of the tables. It would have been easy to mark you as mine."

What the hell was he saying?

It was a threat, and yet his words did something to my insides, dampening my panties.

His warm breath blew again on my skin followed by a deep inhale. "When you walked into the room, you were frightened. I could smell it. I'm here to help."

My nipples grew diamond-hard with each word. I could blame the cool air, but that had only been the start. Inhaling, I turned, facing him.

He took a step back and handed me the bra. "Here, put it on."

Was I disappointed?

Did I want him to say something?

Did I expect him to reach out?

Hell, my mind was too jumbled to know what I expected or wanted. Putting my arms through the straps, with my eyes still locked on his green gaze, my fingers fumbled with the clasp.

"Turn around."

I did. With a quick flick of his fingers, my bra was secure.

"Now, let me see."

No longer thinking about the repercussions of what was happening, I obeyed, a puppet to his rumbling voice as he commanded my movement.

His eyes zeroed in on my breasts, as his fingers ran over

the lace edges, under each cup, and over the underwire. "Can you feel it? I don't want it to poke you."

I shook my head and mumbled, finding talking difficult. My mind was utterly confused as to how I'd gotten to a place where a man whose name I didn't even know was now in my bedroom and touching my breasts.

The man took a step back and handed me the sweatshirt that I'd tossed onto the bed. "Hurry, put this back on."

After I put the sweatshirt on and zipped the suitcase, I stood taller. "How will I know you're close? What if something happens?"

Though his jaw was set, there was something in his gaze, a heat I hadn't seen before.

"Not only will I be close, I'll be certain nothing happens."

"Why?"

"Because the next time your shirt is off, I want to do more than secure a listening device."

My eyes opened wide. It wasn't the answer I expected, yet somehow, in the midst of this crazy night, it reassured me. I didn't know who this man was or why he was helping me.

Hell, I didn't know *if* he was helping me.

Yet wanting me...

That I believed.

That I saw in his expression and heard in his baritone thunder.

Though I didn't want to admit it to even myself, I wanted to be with him again. I wanted to find out what *more than secure a listening device* meant.

"Now, hurry," he said. "They're probably already suspicious."

"Do I...?" I inhaled. "Russ said to not be honest with them."

"I heard him."

"Your advice?"

"Whatever you say will be heard by them, whomever they work for, and me. Nothing is confidential. What's always a good rule of thumb—don't say it or write it if you don't want everyone to know."

"Dr. Carlson." The voice echoed from the first level.

I nodded to the man I didn't know as I opened the door, wheeling my small suitcase. "I'm coming, Officer."

The man reached for my wrist, stopping my exit. His voice rumbled through me as he inhaled again near my neck. "That's better."

"What?"

"You no longer smell of fear. It's something else. Keep thinking about it. Throw them off. Don't let them know you're scared."

"What? I don't know what you mean."

Letting go of my wrist, his finger skimmed my palm. "You smell of desire."

KADER

*L*aurel's scent lingered in the air of her bedroom after she'd switched off the light and walked away, step by step, down the stairs. I hadn't told her not to tell the men about me. I knew it wasn't necessary. My gut may have made me change course with this assignment, but it had also kept me alive through the years.

I trusted it.

And for an unknown reason, I trusted her.

A faith I allotted very few people.

Then why her?

Laurel had already proven herself by simply calling to the men downstairs and not alerting them to my presence. It could have been her attempt to save their lives, but I sensed it was more. She was rightfully scared. And if she knew the depth of the plots to stop her research, her fear would turn to terror. She wasn't ready for that information, not yet. I was still working to pull it all together, but even what I had was too much for her to comprehend. That was not meant to insinuate that she wasn't bright enough to understand. Hell no. It was that from my observation, Laurel saw her work as a way to save people. That's the way good people look at life. The problem was that she wasn't surrounded by good people.

Far from it.

It took an altruistic point of view to have such a narrow scope of focus. Word had gotten out and the bidding was high. Few players in this game were out to help victims of traumatic events. No, their goals were not as lofty. The ability to make people forget selective memories had nefarious potential. Many saw that. Many wanted that.

Others wanted to stop that.

Others wanted to profit from that, no matter the final usage.

The sound of the outside door in Laurel's front room closing echoed through the old house. I took a step toward the window and peered down onto the driveway. My neck straightened as an officer opened the back door of the sedan and Laurel got in. The neighborhood below was dark save for the dotting of porch lights and now the blue LED beams of the car backing onto the street.

Taking a step away from the window, I pulled out my phone and logged onto the app connecting me audibly to the device Laurel was wearing in her bra.

Hell, the fucking white lace and satin threatened to make

me hard by simply holding it. The process had begun when her body was against mine. I'd gotten it under control until I helped her with the damn clasp. When she turned and faced me, the bra and the half globes of her tits in full view, my dick took on a life of its own.

That was something else that was out of character.

I was a man in control of everything—everything. A well-paid whore could fall to her knees and suck me like the professional she was. The sight of her didn't affect me. She just was. Probably beautiful, too much makeup, tits the size of the Rocky Mountains. Pert lips didn't do it for me. I decided when my body reacted, when it needed relief. From start to finish, that professional was simply a means to my end.

My fist could do the same thing, but it rarely did.

Control.

It was what I demanded of myself in every instance.

And now, for some reason, everything seemed different with a woman I barely knew. Laurel was beauty, intellect, and a sweet naïveté all wrapped in the perfect soft package. I tried to keep my mind on the transmitter. Yet as the coarse tips of my fingers traced her bra and the soft skin of her tits...as she allowed me to do that with her big blue eyes looking up at me...I was a fucking goner.

When I'd told her what I could have done, how I could have taken her, it wasn't the first time those thoughts had entered my mind. The second I saw her alone, I envisioned the warmth of her wet pussy strangling my dick. I imagined the sounds she would make in both ecstasy and pain as I filled her, thrust after thrust, giving her more than she could take. In that visualization she came apart screaming my name.

That was why it could never happen.

The whores I hired didn't learn either of my names.

In that fantasy, Laurel did.

That could never happen.

A woman like Dr. Laurel Carlson deserved a better man than I am. She deserved a man with a name. Someone who saw good in this godforsaken world didn't need a man who saw only evil. Currently, this wasn't about a match made in heaven or hell. This was about an assignment and getting it done.

I took a deep breath, adjusted myself, and turned on the Bluetooth in my ear. Her voice came into range. "...exactly do you want me to see at the lab?"

"It's difficult to know what, if anything, is missing..."

Taking the stairs two at a time, I made it to the first level and quietly exited her house. Leaving through the side door I secured the bolt behind me. Creating a key to a lock as old as hers wasn't rocket science. All it took was a small, insertable 360-degree camera and a 3D printer. Hell, it was literally child's play these days and yet most people were unaware. As I made my way to my vehicle, I stayed hidden in the shadows and surveyed the surroundings.

I'd watched from above as Cartwright made his way out of the house and escaped behind a line of tall shrubbery that lined Laurel's yard. The fucker had a key to this house. He might be back. If I didn't think less of him before, I sure as hell did now that he left Laurel to deal with the police by herself. Over the last few days, I'd attached a few discreet cameras on the entrances to her house as well as other locations. There were many different working parts to keep monitored. The video all went to a secure cloud.

I'd watch every inch of footage when I could.

Cartwright could wait. Laurel was my priority. Nothing was happening to her on my watch.

Then again, if I'd been wrong about the identity of those men, it could.

I changed the screen of my phone to keep her heart rate and the GPS visible while at the same time still being able to do further research. Her heart rate was elevated, which under the circumstances was normal. Nevertheless, I wondered if it was because of the situation or because she was doing as I'd advised and keeping her mind off the fear and on desire?

Fuck.

My dick had finally begun to forget, and now that thought alone brought back the rush of circulation.

I changed my thoughts to the two men. I wouldn't hesitate to take them out or even her partner if necessary. Killing was part of my job. I did it without thought or remorse as easily as others did their jobs. One man crunched numbers. I crunched skulls.

If I admitted the complete truth, I had allowed her to go with them to gain information. Things were moving too fucking fast. Being with her audibly would allow me to discover what they found at the lab. I'd been in there more than once and come up empty. Yes, there was information. It wasn't complete.

I also wondered what had been taken and if the authorities had any clues.

Once she found out what they knew or suspected, I'd take her away. There were too many variables with a safe house—one protected by law enforcement anyway. They had rules. I didn't.

I ran my hand over my hair as I navigated the dark city streets. Closer to campus the tall streetlights shone. The audible transmission had gone quiet, yet her heart rate was steady with the GPS moving a few city blocks ahead of me.

Over the course of the last week, this fucking job had snowballed into much more than I signed on to do.

It wasn't all due to circumstance. I'd decided to take this further by altering my plan—something I rarely did.

Fuck that.

Never.

I'd never altered a plan.

That was why I succeeded.

I'd agreed to a job to end the research. That could still happen. My means simply changed.

As I drove, I typed the officers' names into a secure cloud —Peter Stanley and Manes. Indianapolis Metro Police Department—and soon I'd have an answer. I'd know if they were who they claimed.

If they weren't, they'd never make it to the lab.

Another city block passed, and as I came closer to the

campus, the phone on the seat beside me buzzed, meaning that my search had already run its course.

I touched the screen.

Fuck.

The officers' pictures appeared, giving me my answer.

LAUREL

*W*ith each turn onto a new street, speed bump, or stoplight, I mentally mapped out our location, all the while resisting the urge to turn in the back seat, look out the back window, and discover if I could spot the man following us—the one who said he'd follow. I had no reason to trust that man or for that matter, the ones driving me to my lab.

After Russ disappeared from my kitchen, I was having difficulty coming to terms with the issue of trusting anyone.

It seemed that since the night of the gathering, I wasn't sure who deserved it and who didn't.

With the two officers in the front seat, the three of us rode in silence, most likely consumed by our own thoughts. Mine were akin to a turbulent sea, churning with undercurrents and crashing waves. The result was that my mind was adrift in murky, unnavigable water.

I watched the recognizable landmarks of the city pass by, yet I couldn't stay focused. I had so many questions. I should be concerned about the men in the front seat, yet there were too many competing concerns.

What happened to Russ?

Where had he gone?

Why had he left me alone?

Why didn't he want me to talk to the police?

Had he been the one to look inside my purse?

It couldn't have been Officer Manes. He'd been in the doorway until I authorized his entrance. If Russ had left through the back doors, did Officer Manes see him?

With the varying light from the outside streetlights, I removed my wallet from my purse and looked inside. My identification, credit cards, and even the fifty-seven dollars of cash were all present.

Maybe I had opened my purse accidentally, unlatching the clasp as I set it down on my way to the front door. Uncertain of anything, I put my wallet back, confident of only one thing.

I couldn't be sure of anything.

What about Stephanie?

Was she with officers at this moment too?

"Have you contacted Drs. Olsen, Cartwright, and Oaks?" I asked.

"Doctor, Detective Lanky is working on that. Our job was to retrieve you."

"Where will you take me afterward?" I hoped my question would help the man listening.

"We'll wait on orders."

Okay. Not helpful.

If the man was currently watching my heart rate, he had to see it was spiking. With each mile closer to the campus and lab, I became more concerned about what I'd find. Russ's words came back, his incomplete sentences. He'd blamed Dr. Oaks for what was happening, and yet I wasn't sure of the magnitude of that statement.

I ran my moist palms over my jeans, wiping away the perspiration the new set of concerns created. As I did, I felt the hard bump. My flash drive was still in my pocket where I'd placed it earlier when I'd dressed.

Officer Manes turned the vehicle onto the campus. Over the years this intercity campus had grown. What originated as a medical center seventy years ago had grown to so much more. A hidden jewel in the universities of the Midwest, the new buildings, excellent accredited faculty, and increased student body were evidence of the hard work and dedication. I'd been happy to do my research under this university's umbrella.

Now, it felt as if it would end.

I hoped what was happening was simply an interruption and not a terminal diagnosis.

There was too much good that could be done with our compound. The early test trials were encouraging.

According to my watch, it was nearing five in the morning,

yet the sky was still black above the tall lights. Most of the students living on campus were asleep while the faculty and staff didn't arrive for another two hours or more.

That wasn't true of all departments. Some required around-the-clock presence.

Office Manes pulled his car up to a parking space close to the entrance, the one I'd entered daily for years. It was strange to see the parking lot so empty in the morning. I usually arrived after eight. Were it not for my assigned parking space, I'd end up down by the river.

"We're here," Officer Stanley announced.

"I know that I asked earlier," I began, "but can you tell me again what I'm supposed to do here?"

"We can take it slowly," Officer Manes said. "It may be difficult to see the destruction. We just need you to be honest about anything that appears missing."

"Destruction?"

"It's not as bad as it sounds," Officer Stanley said. "After a thorough inventory, we will ask you some questions..."

Be honest.

That was the one thing Russ told me not to be.

Officer Stanley opened his door and a few seconds later was out of the car and opening my door. The cool spring air helped my nerves as I stood in the parking lot, took a deep breath, and looked up at the familiar building. Our offices and lab were on the fifth floor—a restricted area with limited access. Only those people who possessed the right credentials could enter. Even the janitorial crews were vetted.

That brought back what I'd been told, that the break-in was discovered by a custodian. Our custodians knew the protocol. It wasn't to call the police.

Recalling Russ's advice to be untruthful, just as quickly, the advice of the man from my bedroom came to mind. He hadn't told me to lie, while at the same time, he hadn't told me to be truthful. He'd said to remember that nothing was confidential. Whatever I said would rapidly be known by many.

And then he'd offered one more bit of sage advice.

Don't show that I'm scared. Think about something else.

No, he told me what to think about.

Him.

He'd said I smelled of desire.

Had I?

My scattered thoughts went to him, the touch of his coarse fingers on my breasts and the heat in his eyes as he stared down at them, covered only with my bra. Like a bolt of lightning, his gaze did something to me, twisting my mind as well as my body.

It was ludicrous that I was entertaining these thoughts as we rode the elevator up to the fifth floor. It was crazy that a man I'd met three times could affect me the way he did.

The elevator stopped.

"Dr. Carlson, do you have your badge to access the floor?"

"What?"

The doors wouldn't open without the access badge.

Shouldn't they have a way to enter?

They were the police.

"Don't you have other officers up here?" I asked. "They can open the elevator with a button on the outside." I nodded to Officer Manes. "You can call them."

"Doctor, it would be easier if you could simply open it."

I fumbled with my purse, suddenly uncomfortable with this arrangement. "I-I'm not sure if I brought my badge. I wasn't exactly thinking with all that's happened."

Without warning the elevator moved again, descending from where we'd first come.

"What the hell?" Officer Stanley said. "Find your damn badge."

My eyes opened wide as Officer Manes pulled my purse from my grasp, some of the contents spilling to the floor. Thankfully, my badge was secured in a zipper pocket with a special lining. Officer Stanley pushed button after button, yet the elevator continued descending until, with a jerk, it came to an abrupt stop.

All of us looked up at the lighted numbers, curious to see where the elevator had stopped as simultaneously, my purse fell from Officer Manes's grasp.

We hadn't returned to the first-floor entry, the grand hall with chairs and an information desk where we'd entered. No, the elevator had bypassed that stop and continued down to the basement, an area that housed the custodial supplies and the students' lockers. Over the years, I'd only been down here a few times.

As the doors opened it appeared the same as it had been

in the past, dim with antiquated fluorescent lighting and painted cement-block walls. Crouching, I reached down for my purse and wallet from the floor as both men drew guns.

"What...?" My voice faded as I stepped back against the silver wall.

The hallway beyond was empty and eerily quiet, the only noise coming from the hum of the lights. I stumbled and gasped as the wall behind me moved. It wasn't a wall, but an alternative door accessing the loading docks.

I hadn't realized that the elevator could open from both sides. Though I knew this space existed, I'd never been there before.

We all spun. Unlike the front side of the elevator that had two moving doors, the back entrance was one large door, probably easier for loading and unloading. We stood in silence as the entire wall moved slowly to one side. With the first crack, a thick fog leaked in, filling the elevator.

"What's happening?" My question went unanswered.

Oh God, the loading docks were on fire.

I spun to the first doors looking for an escape. It was too late. They were now closed. I too began pushing buttons leading to every floor, trying to get the loading door to close and the elevator to move.

It was as if the elevator had a mind of its own. The panic bubbling inside me erupted in coughs. It wasn't only me. All three of us were coughing yet the door wasn't open enough for even one of us to escape.

After returning their guns to their holsters, the two officers reached for the edge and pried, trying to open it enough for our escape.

While fire had been my first thought, my mind was slow to recognize that whatever was surrounding us wasn't smoke.

There was no odor.

I pressed my lips together, not smelling the fog but tasting it. My nose scrunched.

Vinegar.

This was a type of gas.

I lowered my face, covering my nose and mouth with the neck of my sweatshirt as my throat burned and lungs grew tight.

Was this what it was like to suffocate?

My eyes began to water as tears leaked down my cheeks. The moisture added to my now-blurry vision. Through the gas, I could barely see the men at my sides. The chemical affected my entire body as I gasped for much-needed oxygen. The lack of essential elements made the small elevator spin, not literally, yet I crouched lower with my hand on the floor and closed my eyes, certain that if I didn't, I would fall.

The air was clearer near the floor because like heat, the gas rose.

I tried to inhale.

There were voices. Perhaps it was the officers—I couldn't be sure of anything. In my utter confusion their words lost meaning.

Help.

I needed help. We all needed help.

I wasn't thinking about their guns or what had happened. My concerns were limited to breathing and an escape.

Through squinted eyes, I watched as the door continued to move. The process of opening didn't cause the gas to dissipate. On the contrary, it was thicker than before, descending toward the floor. I wanted to move forward, yet my body wasn't taking orders from my brain. Placing one hand in front of the other, I tried to crawl. My arms and legs weren't responding.

A man's scream bounced off the metal walls as the clank of something reverberated beside me on the floor. Opening my eyes, I tried to reach out. A bright flash of light penetrated the fog milliseconds before something else hit the floor. Forcing my hands to move, I reached out, my fingers contacting what felt like the material of a cheap suit.

The officers were now on the floor beside me.

My stomach revolted as queasiness blossomed, yet I didn't have the energy to carry through and vomit.

Overwhelming exhaustion changed my goal. If only I could lower my head to the floor...

I needed sleep.

The world went black.

LAUREL

*C*hoking...coughing...

  My lungs burned as my body convulsed, racked with coughs waking me to this new world.

Where was I?

How long had I been asleep?

I blinked, my eyelids fluttering, finding nothing beyond. Even my hand before my face was invisible. The vision of darkness was the same whether my eyes were opened or closed. It wasn't unusual when waking to have a sense of disorientation, but this was more.

I opened my eyes wider, fearful that I'd lost my sight.

It was rare for darkness to be the true absence of light. The human eye could adjust to the dimmest illumination. Yet this was different. As I blinked away moisture and rubbed aside the irritants gathered in the corners of my eyes, I found myself surrounded by true and utter blackness.

My pulse increased as I ran my palm over the surface of where I'd awakened. The blankets were soft under my touch. I'd been sufficiently warm under their protection; however, the same couldn't be said about the room—the location.

I had no point of reference, no way to fathom where I was or how I'd gotten here. I couldn't remember exactly...

Though my instinct was to panic, my analytical mind sought clues.

More coughs came bubbling from my chest as I sat taller. With my neck straightening, I used the senses available to me. The stagnant air surrounding me reeked with mustiness, as if filled with dust and the odor of decay—not that of biological remains. No, this offending scent reminded me of my grandparents' basement when I was a child.

The space beneath their home had been a large concrete room filled with cardboard boxes left to disintegrate over time. I pictured it in my mind's eye. There were metal shelves that lined the walls while towers of plastic and cardboard containers filled with precious, priceless memories were piled about. As an adult I would see it for what it was—a mess in need of a dumpster and a haven for insects and vermin. As a child I saw it differently. It was a playground with limitless possibilities for our imagination. During our visits, my sister and I would explore, going down the dark steps with a flashlight in hand. We'd find a secret corner and make up ghost stories, each trying to frighten the other.

What I wouldn't do for that flashlight now.

The odor currently hanging in the air fit perfectly with my memory.

In our research we'd confirmed the role that the olfactory process played in memories. That sense was one of the strongest triggers.

Touch.

Beneath me was a bed—a mattress at least—with sheets, blankets, and pillows.

Taste.

My mouth was dry as if consuming too much alcohol while at the same time tasted sour.

Hearing.

I sat perfectly still. The thump of my heartbeat and inhalation were the only audible clues in the near silence.

"Hello?" I called into the darkness. My voice echoed off what I could assume were cement walls or walls made of concrete blocks. I called out again, listening to the reverberation of my voice, determining the room was taller than it was wide.

A small room.

The memory of the elevator came back.

The foul-tasting gas.

The police officers that I suspected weren't.

What if...?

The temperature dropped or perhaps it was that my circulation slowed at the possibility.

What if those men had me?

Could that be where I was?

Why?

Like a game of Tetris, different fragmented memories bombarded my thoughts, each coming faster and needing a place to rest.

The phone call.

Russ.

The police.

The man.

My hands immediately went to my bra, trying to feel the device he'd placed.

Was it still there?

What if they found it?

I was still wearing the sweatshirt I'd put on during the night. Reaching beneath the hem, I confirmed that the white bra was still in place as were my blue jeans. I stretched out my legs and reached into one of the pockets.

"No." The pocket was empty.

Fumbling with the material, I reached into the other side and let out a long breath. Digging deeper, the small flash drive was again in my grasp.

My mind went back to the transmitter. "Can you hear me?" I asked in a whisper. "I think I need help. I don't know where I am." The confession brought back a bit of the panic, yet that wouldn't help me be found. I inhaled and exhaled, pushing emotions away. "I think I'm in a basement or cellar. It's cool and very dark."

For a moment I sat waiting.

For what?

I wasn't sure. The transmitter couldn't talk back to me.

Shaking my head, I wrapped the bed's blanket around my shoulders, deciding it was up to me to understand my surroundings. I'd relay any information I could.

Moving to the edge of the bed, I placed my feet on the floor. As I did, I realized my shoes were gone or at least had been removed. The only things separating my feet from the cool floor were the socks I'd put on during the night.

With one hand on the bed, I walked around its perimeter, estimating its size. It wasn't large enough to be a king or small enough to be a twin. The opposite long side was against a cold, rough wall as also was the head. The headboard was metal—brass maybe. It was difficult to tell. Whatever material it was made of felt cool to the touch. Following the edge of the room, I moved. Nothing obstructed my path—no other furniture or plumbing. The final corner, took me to the fourth wall. Not far from the foot of the bed. I sighed as I found what must be the door.

A spark of excitement jolted my system. "I found a door," I said to the device.

The handle was a simple knob that turned easily in my hand. It didn't matter which direction I turned it or if I pushed or pulled, the door itself didn't budge—it did nothing more than rattle upon its hinges. I reached up and down, feeling for those. If they were on the inside, I could remove the pins.

They weren't.

The door was obviously held in place by an exterior lock or more than one. I also assumed that the door was trimmed in some kind of rubber or something to keep the light at bay.

My gut instinct was to beat upon the barrier and scream at the top of my lungs. The thought that kept me still and mute was the uncertainty of whom I'd summon.

Was it better to be in here alone or out there with someone?

When I'd awakened, I'd thought of my mystery man, hoping he'd saved me.

Walking back to the bed with my hand out for guidance, I found my target and sat near the foot. "Are you here?" I asked quietly, knowing he couldn't respond.

With each passing minute, my needs became more urgent. I was thirsty but mostly I needed a bathroom. Those weren't the only causes of my rising anxiety.

I started to worry about my friends and coworkers as well as the man I didn't know.

What if they were all being held like me?

Who would go to this extreme?

"Oh," I gasped, recalling that Stephanie had said she was also being taken to the lab.

I stood, creating a track as I paced and worried.

Russ, Eric, Stephanie, and the mystery man.

What if the mystery man no longer held the ability to listen to my transmissions?

If he'd been stopped, then someone else heard my description of this place. That was what he'd said. He'd said that nothing I said was confidential. It could be heard by others.

Had I been wrong to talk and describe my surroundings?

I couldn't be sure of anything.

Time continued to pass with no way to discern its length.

Seconds.

Minutes.

Hours.

There was no clock or watch to track its speed or duration. The sun or moon was blocked from my view. I paced and sat. Sat and lay down. I contemplated my options if no one came to me.

Just as I was about to do the unthinkable and empty my bladder onto the concrete floor, as I stood determined with my mission at hand, I stopped dead in my tracks. Newfound alarm circulated throughout my bloodstream. My once-calmed heart raced, skyrocketing my pulse to an unhealthy rate as the distinctive click and swish of moving locks came from the other side of the door.

With my bladder forgotten, my empty stomach twisted. I took one step and then another backward, my eyes focused toward the sounds, toward the door. I wrapped the blanket tighter around me and continued to move until my shoulders collided with the far cement-block wall.

I held my breath, my eyes opened wide, as the door opened outward. The swish of something over the concrete confirmed my theory that the door was lined to keep out light.

The area beyond the doorway grew brighter than the room.

As the light grew, so did relief at the reassurance of sight.

Appearing before me was a silhouette devoid of definition. It was a shadow, an outline of a man, his form practically filling the space. His wide shoulders almost touched on both sides, while his head was near the top. The form before me appeared solid, a statue carved of stone.

I knew before he spoke.

I knew it was him.

The visual confirmation flooded me with relief.

"Oh, thank God, it's you."

KADER

I shook my head. Her response was nothing like I'd expected. "Best not to make assumptions."

With the room still dark, from the hallway I had the advantage. Laurel's forehead furrowed as she analyzed my comment. Her eyes grew wide and she pulled the blanket tighter around her body. With each passing second her expression grew tenser, her relief giving way to confusion.

Finally, she spoke. "What do you mean?"

If only she knew how comical her question was, but she didn't.

She didn't know anything about me, about the man who took her. She couldn't. She also didn't understand her worth at this moment.

I took a step back and gestured toward the hallway.

"You've been asleep for over ten hours. If you promise to stay quiet, there's a bathroom down the hall that you can use."

Laurel continued her stare as if I hadn't spoken. "You didn't answer my question."

Lifting my arm, I gripped the side of the doorframe. "I don't repeat offers." Reaching with my other hand for the door, I began to close it.

"Wait," she called as she stepped forward. "I-I do need..."

As she came closer, the dim light of the hallway brought color back to her blue eyes. They stayed fixed on mine. The simple gesture had me off-balance.

Most women—hell, men too—avoided looking at me, seeing me. They would mumble a response and keep their eyes averted. It was as if they sensed how dangerous I could be—what I was capable of doing. Perhaps they reasoned that if they didn't truly see me, they might be safe.

That wasn't always the case.

The sense of dread that covered me in a cloud worked to my advantage. It hid me from the masses. I wore it willingly like a cloak; its presence allowed me to exist outside people's perception. Good or evil, it didn't matter. People in general didn't want to remember me. To their consciousness I was a ghost or figment of their imagination. They avoided me because their subconscious knew the truth.

I wasn't a ghost.

I was the boogeyman.

The invisibility it offered was helpful in my line of work. It wasn't often that I came face-to-face with an assignment. When I did, our association was most often short-lived.

For me, conversations weren't accomplished by speaking. They occurred behind a screen and keyboard. Kader was faceless—the opposite of the truth.

Rarely did I have the desire to speak, to talk.

That was all different with Laurel.

From the first time I saw her picture, she fascinated me. From the screen of my computer, she looked at me. I felt it.

My mind and experience told me I was wrong. Surely when faced with the actuality that the mythical creature living under children's beds was real, Laurel Carlson would do as others did and look away.

The night of the gathering had been her first opportunity. I'd stayed hidden until that night. Entering the banquet hall, I told myself she wasn't different. And then she turned. I expected her to turn away just as quickly. It didn't happen. From across the room our gazes met.

I gave her another chance to sense the reality of my nature. She was a woman alone in a dimly lit hall. Yet when faced with me, she didn't blink. She didn't frighten. She never looked away.

I wasn't certain why Laurel's reaction was different.

She should sense the danger that others did, but with each encounter it was the opposite.

In a short time, I'd become addicted. Having her bright blue orbs looking at me was like a drug. Of course, I couldn't allow her to see me, the real me, just as she would never call out my real name.

Some things were impossible.

But fuck, I was off-kilter. This assignment had me hoping. A man like me didn't hope. I was in control. I made things happen. Hope was for those who refused to take action. I took action.

Laurel came to a stop before me, her blue eyes speaking more than her lips. They did something to me. Having her look at me made me want the impossible.

I swallowed and after a nod, I tilted my head to my left.

When she took a step, I lowered my arm, blocking her path.

"What?" she asked.

Her question held too many possibilities. Keeping those thoughts at bay, I said, "No noise."

"Okay."

"No, Laurel. I want to hear you tell me you won't make noise. There needs to be no confusion on this."

"Will you tell me what's happening?"

"Eventually."

"Am I safe here with you or not?"

"Well, that depends."

"On what?"

"If you can follow simple instructions. Come on, Doc, you're a brilliant woman. Right now, I need your word that you won't do anything stupid like scream or try to find a way out."

The expression on her face said she wanted to argue or at least get more answers. The minute bouncing of her body broadcast that she had a more pressing issue, and currently, I was the only one keeping her from that.

She lifted her chin. "Where are we?"

I shook my head. "Not what I said."

She straightened her neck. "I will be quiet."

My arm rose higher, keeping my grasp of the doorjamb high enough for her to pass. Almost. In order to enter the hallway, Laurel had to duck, lowering her haughty chin to pass.

The hallway she'd entered, the direction she'd gone, had one other door. There was no possible way she could escape. The path led her only to the small bathroom.

It wasn't much—a stand-up corner shower, sink, and toilet. I'd added some towels and basic toiletries. It wasn't like I had any idea of what a woman needed. Thankfully, I grabbed the suitcase she'd packed. I recalled watching her throw a few things in there last night or more accurately, early this morning.

The bathroom was a hell of a lot cleaner than when I'd moved into this dump, and bonus, now the water worked. It wasn't the Ritz or even her antique house. It was a sight ready for demolition on the street level, run-down and almost beyond repair. That was why I kept my activity to the lower level. One day, I'd leave it abandoned or sell it to some crook of a house flipper.

Right now, we needed a place to stay and it served my purpose.

The door to the bathroom closed. For a few seconds the handle rattled. No doubt she was looking for a lock—there wasn't one. Even if there had been one, locks were for honest people. They didn't stop men like me.

Kidnapping wasn't my usual gig; nevertheless, it didn't take a genius IQ to know the basics.

Keep the asset hidden and establish control.

The reason I didn't kidnap as a rule was because it was fucking easier to simply kill people.

I needed to remember that before I changed up another assignment midstream.

Flipping a switch, I brought light to the hallway. She'd been left in the dark for a reason—her damn eyes. It was difficult to predict how the gas affected them and how long it would take for it to leave her system. It made sense that darkness would give her time to heal and adjust.

Now, based on the strip of light coming from below the bathroom door, she'd turned it on in there. Since I couldn't hear her say otherwise, I reasoned she must be doing all right.

Crossing my arms over my chest, I waited for her to exit.

It took some time, but she finally did.

The blanket was still wrapped around her and again, her head was held high. "I need water. The stuff coming out of that faucet smells. I doubt it's safe for consumption."

"You're probably right. Lead pipes and all." I tilted my

head the other direction. "I got you some water and food. Your suitcase is this way too."

I turned, leading the way, when her small hand reached out, landing on my lower arm.

"What the hell?" I asked, pulling my arm away.

The sleeves of my shirt were lowered to my wrists to keep her from seeing what was beneath. I spun toward her. "Touching me is forbidden. Don't try it again."

Her cheeks paled as she pulled her hand back, clenching it to her chest.

My mind told me she didn't actually feel what was beneath. Nevertheless, that didn't change my reaction or soften my reprimand.

"I-I'm sorry," Laurel said. "I wanted to get your attention."

"Then speak. I can fucking hear."

"Who are you?"

"Stop asking questions and follow me."

Yes, I caught the irony.

My boots clipped the concrete as we walked. The hallway opened to a large room, one that spanned the length of the house above. I'd found a few furnishings here and there. Since I hadn't planned on having a guest, none of it was very nice. There was an old wooden table with three chairs, a worn sofa I'd found at a used furniture shop, a tattered recliner, and a small refrigerator taking a portion of the room.

The rest was separated by a makeshift wall I'd created. The wood frame was covered with Plexiglas instead of drywall. I'd done that to keep an eye on the entire space. Now,

I could keep an eye on Laurel too. She could be in the one side. I could be working on the other, all the while with the ability to keep an eye on her.

Kidnapping 101: avoid letting the asset out of your sight and if you do, keep her secured.

Beyond the Plexiglas was my work space. Tables constructed to create desks were covered in computer equipment. One of the three monitors was devoted to surveillance feeds. This setup paled in comparison to what I had on my ranch, but it was sufficient to complete this assignment.

I pointed to the table. "Sit down."

"What's over there?" She pointed toward my computers.

"That's my space. It's off-limits."

As she sat, her gaze scanned the room. "You have a lot of rules."

"I do. Rules keep you safe."

"Is that your goal, to keep me safe?"

"Fuck," I said as I opened the refrigerator to the groceries I'd bought. "My goals have changed." Taking a water bottle out, I placed it on the table. "There are ten more. You're probably thirsty."

Laurel didn't answer. Instead, she reached for the water, twisted the cap, and began to drink. Not drink—gulp. She'd downed over half of the bottle when she began coughing again.

I'd heard her coughing on the transmitter when she'd first awakened. I would have gone to her, but I wasn't here. I'd been out looking for answers.

"Slow down. I didn't bring you here to have you choke to death." Next, I removed a premade Greek salad.

"Why did you bring me here?" Her eyes were still moving about the room. "And where is here? I can't see a window or even a door. What time is it? How do we get out?"

Ignoring her litany of questions, I placed the salad on the table. "I need to find out what you like to eat." I opened the lid and handed her a small plastic envelope with a plastic fork and knife. "I saw one of these in your refrigerator, so I figured you liked it."

What the hell?

He saw it in my refrigerator.

The man leaned against the see-through wall and crossed his arms over his chest. Without giving it conscious thought, I did as I'd done before and scanned him from toe to head. He was still wearing the boots, jeans, and black thermal that he'd worn at my house. When our eyes met, I fought the urge to look away. The intensity of his green stare was both comforting and disconcerting. The odd combination knotted my empty stomach.

Time stood still for a second or two as we both remained silent.

Finally, he nodded toward the table. "Eat."

Reaching for the small foil packet of dressing, I asked, "How many times have you been in my house?" Ripping the top, I waited for his answer as I simultaneously drizzled the vinaigrette over the romaine lettuce, onions, peppers, tomatoes, and cucumbers. The olives and feta cheese were in separate containers. My hands began to tremble as I mixed everything together. I hadn't realized the voracity of my hunger until food was at my fingertips.

It was as if nothing else mattered. Even in this odd situation, primal needs were the first that required fulfillment.

As I stuffed a large forkful of lettuce and olives into my mouth, a noise escaped my lips. It was a groan or a moan. I wasn't sure. All I knew was the salad was delicious.

The man said I'd been asleep for over ten hours.

Was he counting the time I'd been awake in that room too?

Either way it was now afternoon or evening.

I looked around the top of the walls for a window to judge the daylight. There were two, both covered with plywood. I should be worried, yet at the moment, consuming the food before me was my paramount concern.

Eating more salad, Maslow's hierarchy of needs came to mind. A simple psychological theory, it states how physiological needs such as food, water, warmth, and rest must be met before moving up the pyramid.

The next level was safety.

I looked back at the covered windows.

Safety.

I wasn't ready to think about that.

Food first.

After a few more bites and some more water, I looked over at the man. "You haven't answered me."

"I thought I told you to stop asking questions."

My head shook as I stabbed the fork into the salad. "I can't. It's what I do." I took a bite and swallowed. "My house..."

"Over the last two weeks, multiple times."

"I should have listened to my dad and had an alarm system installed."

His lips quirked. "That wouldn't have stopped me. It also wouldn't stop people you welcomed into your front door or ones who have keys. Basically, your house could second as Grand Central Station. Even your neighbor comes and goes."

I knew about Mrs. Beeson. We had an understanding. However, hearing him casually discuss people coming and going from my private residence chilled my skin. I pulled the blanket back to my shoulders.

Although I was eating and had the basic needs met, that was only the first level of the hierarchy. The more he said, the less I felt safe. No, the real issue was that unbeknownst to me, I hadn't been safe for some time. I tugged the blanket tighter. "I knew about Mrs. Beeson. How did I not know that you'd been there?"

"People like you never do."

"Like *me*?" I asked, leaning back on the chair. With food and water in my stomach and the use of the bathroom, my mind was now filled with questions. I wanted information.

Reaching for another chair, the man spun it on one leg and

straddled the back. His long legs came to rest on either side as his arms folded over the top. His biceps bulged against the black material of his thermal shirt. Unlike in my bedroom last night, the top two buttons of his shirt were undone, revealing the edge of colorful ink that must cover his chest as well as his arms. I watched his Adam's apple bob and jaw strain as if he were deciding what he should say.

In the light of the room with the way he was seated, confidence radiated from him while at the same time there was a casual comfort.

At ease could be a good description.

Although this situation was inconceivable and I was still unsure about anything and everything, his attitude comforted me. Maybe it was a false sense of security. I couldn't be sure.

His green stare bore into me as his voice reverberated through the cement room. "People like *you*..." He emphasized the word. "...trust others. You see good not bad. You don't look for clues because you trust that everyone around you lives by your moral standards."

"You don't know me."

He stood and took a step closer. I leaned farther back to maintain eye contact. One more step and he was right beside me. The proximity washed away my earlier sense of comfort. "What?" I asked, suddenly nervous.

He reached out and ran the pad of his finger over my cheek as my neck stiffened.

"I thought you said no touching."

"I said you can't touch me. I've already touched you." His

finger moved lower to my jaw, neck, and collarbone. With a flick of his wrist he lowered the blanket. "Maybe I should check on that transmitter."

Quickly, I scooted the chair away, the screech against the cement floor cutting through the musty air. I stood as the blanket fell to the floor. "What are you doing?"

He moved the chair, the only obstacle between us. "I'm showing you how wrong your outlook is."

We moved in unison until the back of my legs collided with the sofa. With each step my pulse ticked higher and my breathing grew shallower. His stare was like a laser to my skin. Even though he wasn't touching me, I felt him, the way his fingers had skimmed my breasts.

With equal parts anticipation and fear, my nipples drew tighter beneath my bra and sweatshirt.

I stood taller. In my bare feet I was easily at a twelve-inch deficit to the man towering above me. "Stop."

Again his finger skirted my cheek. "You think I'm a good man. You said that when I opened the door. You said you were glad it was me."

"I-I think...I don't know you, but if it was you or those fake police, I was glad it was you."

His hands skimmed my arms, flittering over the sleeves of my sweatshirt. "How do you know they were fake?"

"Because you saved me from them."

"What if I didn't?" His hands continued to roam just beyond my skin, a ghostly touch to the sleeves. "What if I'm the bad man?"

"You're trying to scare me."

"Or I'm telling you the truth. That's what I mean about people like you. You can't see the evil because it's not who you are." He reached for the bottom hem of my sweatshirt. "I'm going to remove this shirt."

"No." My voice was shaky as my head moved from side to side.

"I want to check that transmitter."

"I don't believe you."

The man forced a smile, one that didn't match his eyes. "You're right, I lied."

"You lied?"

"I want to see your soft tits."

"I-I..."

"Tell me, are you frightened?" He leaned closer and inhaled.

It was weird and intriguing at the same time.

When I didn't respond, he began to lift my shirt. "Or are you turned on?"

"What? No." I pushed his hand away and secured the hem in my grasp. "Fine. You proved your point. You're not good."

"Oh, Laurel, you're mistaken. I'm very good."

My lips pursed as I stood straighter. "Whatever. Now back the hell up."

"What's to stop me from taking you on the sofa, right here, right now?"

The dusty air caught in my lungs as my knees grew weak. I was no match for this man, but I sure as hell wasn't going down without a fight. Letting go of my sweatshirt, I lifted my palm inches from his chest. "Me. I said no."

"And you think that's enough?"

"It should be."

"Laurel, this isn't a should-be game. This is life or death." His head shook slowly. "For this arrangement to work, you need to leave the directions up to me. And when I give them, you listen and obey. You're playing a high-stakes poker game with *Go Fish* skills. This is out of your league." He took one step back.

I let out a long breath.

Why had he done that?

I'd felt safe with him, but now I didn't know exactly what I was feeling.

I reached for my own hand. "If you want the transmitter, I'll go in the bathroom and take off my bra."

"I don't want the transmitter. I want you to realize this is serious shit. I haven't determined who those men were at your house last night or who they worked for. I also can't figure out what they wanted." His shoulder shrugged. "They took you to the university, and yet there wasn't a break-in."

"What do you mean?"

"I wanted to see what happened at your lab for myself. I went to the university while you were unconscious." He turned around and resumed his backward straddle of the chair. "I don't believe that there was a break-in. Nothing appeared out of place."

"I don't understand." I moved back to the chair where I'd

been sitting and lowered myself to the seat. "How did you get in? It's restricted."

For a moment, he pressed his lips together and stared. Finally, he spoke, "The security at the university isn't as infallible as you want to believe. Entering the floor undetected wasn't the problem. I entered each area. The problem that concerns me is that the labs and offices were all closed, as in no one was there. Lights out."

"I have so many questions. Are you sure that no one was there?" I asked. "It's a Tuesday."

He glanced at the band on his wrist. "For a little while longer."

"What about Stephanie?" I shook my head. "What about all of them? Russ, Eric..." My voice trailed away. Before he could speak, I added one more. "No, first, before any of that, tell me who you are and why I'm here."

He ran his long fingers over his light brown hair as if to smooth unruly locks. That wasn't necessary; most of his hair was secured at the nape of his neck as it had been the night of the gathering. There were a few rogue strands hanging near his cheeks, reaching just past his jaw. They were lighter than the rest, contrasting his darker facial hair.

If they had his intensely green eyes, this man could be the perfect combination of Charlie Hunnam, Brad Pitt, and a younger Nikolaj Coster-Waldau.

Strikingly handsome.

I took a deep breath. "I've stayed quiet. If I scream will anyone hear me?"

"Hard to say. Don't do it."

"You are...?"

"I told you. I'm the man who kept you breathing."

"The gas in the elevator...that was you, right?" I asked.

He nodded.

"So you're also the person responsible for me being unconscious."

He shrugged. "Seemed like the better alternative."

"Do you have a name?"

"Doesn't everyone?"

I crossed my arms over my chest and pressed my lips together.

"I'm called Kader."

I mulled his answer over in my mind. "That's unusual."

He nodded. "It means destiny in Turkish."

"Isn't Destiny a woman's name?" Maybe it was my attempt to lighten the mood after what had just happened near the couch. My cheeks rose at my question because there was nothing remotely feminine about the man sitting across the table from me.

"It's my job."

"What is?"

"Determining people's destiny. Like yours, for instance."

So much for a lighter mood. "Like those men?"

"Eventually."

His answer sent a chill down my spine. "What is my destiny?"

"Right now, you're alive and safe."

I let out a breath as I looked around the room and recalled the scene from minutes earlier. "Am I? Where are we?"

"You're in hiding."

I stood again and walked around the room, taking in the furniture and stark concrete walls. "Is this like a safe house or something?"

He shrugged his broad shoulders. "Or something. It's a house and you're safe."

"Where's the door?"

Kader tilted his head toward the area with the computers. I hadn't noticed it before, but in the far corner there was a door.

"Don't go near it."

"This is insane." My hands slapped my hips. "I need my phone. I need to call Russ." I remembered Stephanie again. "Those men at my house. They weren't really policemen, were they?"

"You knew that as soon as they wanted your badge to enter the fifth floor."

That was when it was confirmed. The first clue was after I gave more thought to the break-in being discovered by one of our custodians and reported to the police, not Dr. Olsen.

When I didn't respond, he continued, "I took pictures of their fake identifications. Unfortunately, they weren't carrying any other forms of ID. I placed trackers in their wallets, ones they won't know about. If they go back to their headquarters, I'll know more. I could have done more; however, those men weren't my goal. I want higher up. I want to know who gave them the orders to take you to the lab."

My mind wasn't on those men. It was something else I recalled. "Stephanie," I said, my words coming faster, "she's my assistant. I spoke to her last night, or this morning. She said the police had called her too. She was going to be taken to the lab." My hands resumed shaking. "If it wasn't broken into and she wasn't there...Kader, what happened to her?"

KADER

*T*his assignment wasn't snowballing out of control. It was a fucking avalanche.

When I took the assignment, I'd completed a background check on Laurel's assistant as well as everyone else who worked in the labs and offices. For her position, Stephanie Stone was overly qualified. I supposed that went with the territory. After all, even assisting on something as advanced as their research and development required more than a high school diploma. Stephanie was a dissertation defense away from her PhD.

"I have cameras on the fifth floor of your building at the university," I said. "Last night, Stephanie was the last to leave the fifth floor. I didn't witness any unusual behavior—nothing that stood out." My head moved from side to side. "I've been a little preoccupied with you, those police impersonators, Cartwright, and Olsen to track down every supporting member of your team."

Laurel's brow wrinkled with concern. "What about Russ and Eric?"

"Off the radar."

"Stephanie is more important than a supporting member, and she said she received the same call. What if the men who went to her have her?"

Not my problem. I didn't say that.

"Give me my phone," Laurel said, reaching out her hand. "I'll call her."

"It would be better if you also stayed under the radar for a while longer."

Laurel stood and walked from the table to the sofa, turned around, and retraced her steps. With her forefinger curled over her chin and the creases of her forehead growing deeper in contemplation, she continued to pace. After a few more treks, she stopped and turned to me. "You're going to take me home, right? You don't plan on me staying here, do you?" Her nose scrunched as she spoke.

She was fucking right. This place stank, literally. What she didn't know was that it was a hell of a lot better than it had been when I got here. When something starts at negative ten on a one-to-ten scale, one is pretty fucking fantastic.

"No to taking you home. Yes to staying here."

"I'm not staying. I need to meet this..." Her hands gestured in circles. "...whatever it is, head-on."

The pressure grew as I clenched my teeth. I wasn't accustomed to explaining my rationale to anyone. When you worked and lived alone, there wasn't much explaining necessary.

I stood. "You will stay here. I want to trust you, but I'm not giving you a chance to escape. It's too dangerous."

"You want to trust *me*? What if I'm not sure I can trust you?"

"Right now, that is irrelevant."

It was Laurel's turn to narrow her gaze. "Just what the hell do you think you're going to do to keep me here?"

"I think I'm going stay between you and the door to the stairs when I'm here. You're not getting past me or through that door."

"This is...kidnapping," she said as she slapped her hips. "It's illegal and wrong."

Her reasoning made me scoff. "Dr. Carlson, if you haven't already figured it out, illegal activity is what I do."

For a moment she stared as if not comprehending my statement. Instead of questioning what I'd said, she moved her now-fisted hands to her hips. "And when you're not here?"

I nodded toward the bedroom down the hallway. "In there."

Her lips pursed before her head began shaking. "Absolutely not. If this place catches on fire, I'd be trapped. It's not safe."

"You're right. If you're the praying type, I suggest you pray for no fire."

"I won't do it."

"Suit yourself. You can always hope for rain."

"No, I'm not talking about praying. I won't stay here locked in that room. When you leave, you're taking me with you. And you're taking me home."

"Sorry, Doc." I wasn't, but it was the expected response. "You'll go to the bedroom if I have to put you over my shoulder and carry you." I shrugged. "It's basically how you got in there in the first place. And if you do anything to attempt to leave, including yelling..." I lifted my brows. "I'll put you over my knee."

"Excuse me? This is crazy. You are crazy."

"What's crazy is thinking that you are safer out there than in here."

"No one out there threatened to carry me over their shoulder or punish me like I'm a child."

I reached again for her shoulders, my fingers squeezing just enough to focus her attention. I hadn't planned to say this much, but it seemed clear that if I didn't convince her of the danger outside, she wouldn't stop arguing.

"Tell me why you think your world imploded," I said, hoping to get her to concentrate on what was occurring beyond these walls. "Think about all that has happened. Don't brush the instances under the rug and pretend that two men didn't just try to get information from you and then do...who knows what to you if given the chance. Don't act like your lab isn't mysteriously shut down. What about Olsen? Why is he suddenly missing? What about your partner? Why did he abandon you? Laurel, look at the bigger picture—the world beyond here."

She swayed within my grasp as her cheeks paled. "I think...I need to sit down."

Letting go of her shoulders, I directed her to the sofa. "Do you want more water?"

"No, I want my life back."

I shook my head. "That's not happening anytime soon."

More like never.

She closed her eyes again, let out a long breath, and leaned back on the sofa's tattered cushions.

The scene was wrong. Laurel Carlson shouldn't be in this dump—she deserved better. Nevertheless, being here was better than what was supposed to happen.

Her eyes opened, the cobalt blue zeroed in on me. "This has to be about the formula. But why now?"

I sat beside her, giving her space. The worn springs sagged under my weight. Exhaling, I leaned forward, placing my elbows on my knees and held my chin. "That gathering last week..."

"Yes," she said as she too leaned forward.

I took in a deep breath. "The purpose of that gathering wasn't to assemble investors who would help you continue your research."

Her head moved. "No, you're wrong. That was why. For weeks or maybe months before the gathering, we—Russ and I

—had numerous discussions and meetings with both Eric and Dr. Oaks. The university determined that additional funding was needed—"

"Laurel," I said, interrupting her, "did you believe what was said? Investors? What about grants?"

"I-I applied for a few over the years. The problem was that I couldn't put into writing the exact nature of our research. It's classified."

Narrowing my eyes, I reached for her chin until the blue was again shining my way. "Who told you not to pursue the grants?"

She shrugged. "I think it was a group decision."

"Think about it. This work is your baby. Didn't you question the need to share even a part of it with a group of people? It's obvious that you trust the people you work with, but dig down deep..."

Not fighting my touch, she sighed as her lids fluttered shut.

"Did you feel good about the gathering?" I asked, again keeping her chin in place.

Her head shook in my grasp.

"Why?"

"I don't like public appearances. I didn't want to be there."

"Tell me more."

She swallowed. "I felt on display, not just me, but my work —our work." Her eyes opened. "Russell—Dr. Cartwright's and mine."

"What else?"

"There were too many people and we said too much."

Letting go of her chin, I nodded. "It's not your fault, none of this. What was said Friday night didn't matter. More information than what was discussed had already been shared long before the gathering."

"What are you talking about?"

"I found a secure email sent out through the university servers."

"No, that's crazy. I'm copied on all correspondence."

I let out a long breath. "Not on this one. As I said, it was secure."

"Then how did you find it?"

Instead of explaining the how, I told her what it contained. "The email discussed specifics about the potential usage of the drug once patented. It even touted the results from the limited clinical trials."

"No." She stood, her expression a mixture of shock and disappointment. "That's all classified confidential. No one should..."

"The email garnered the wrong attention," I said. "That gathering was for one reason. It was a ruse to secure a buyer for the formula and resulting compound—scare the potential buyers into making a move. Bids were already high, but after that little show, they skyrocketed." Her lips paled as she pressed them together. I went on, "A deposit has already been paid with much more offered to stop your research at any cost."

"What does that mean—*any cost?*"

"Laurel, there's a price on your head, one that has been accepted."

LAUREL

*S*itting on the bed, with my head against the headboard and my back supported by pillows, I stared at the walls surrounding me and recounted the concrete blocks. Their pattern was like a jigsaw puzzle made completely out of rectangular pieces. I'd been right about the higher ceiling. The difference between now and when I'd awakened was that now I had a button—a remote—to turn on and off the one light bulb hanging from a high rafter. I couldn't stop thinking about my earlier conversation with Kader.

If there was a price on my head, was there also one on Russell's?

That was only one of the questions I had floating around in the mess that was my brain. Ever since the moment Kader said that someone wanted me dead, my thoughts were muddled by his revelation.

He'd left the building—safe house—a while ago.

After he dropped that bomb, he left me sitting on the old sofa and walked to the other side of the plastic wall. A few moments later, he came back with my suitcase. I never asked how he'd gotten it or what exactly happened to the two fake police officers. There were too many questions to keep them all prioritized.

Taking the suitcase to the bedroom, I'd opted to do something, anything that I could do. The last twenty-four hours had seemed like a lifetime and after my hunger was fulfilled, I noticed the lingering scent of the gas emanating from my pores, surrounding me like a cloud. With very little currently in my control, brushing my teeth and showering were two things I could accomplish.

I'd done my best to not drink the faucet's water as I brushed. Instead, I'd used the water from the water bottle to rinse. I had no choice with the shower. At least the smelly water was warm. Hot would be an exaggeration, but lukewarm was better than cold.

After I was done, wearing yoga pants, a t-shirt, and socks with wet combed-out hair, I'd made my way back to the bigger room. When I entered, Kader was on the other side of the plastic wall, staring at three screens as his fingers alternated between clicking the keyboard and moving a mouse.

The direction in which he was seated allowed me to see him—his striking face and broad shoulders—but not what was on the screens.

At first I wasn't sure if he knew I was there. He appeared

to be enthralled with whatever information he was gathering. His eyes stared as his chiseled jaw clenched. The length of his brow varied as he turned from one screen to the other. His wide chest expanded and contrasted with exaggerated breaths. When he did, his shirt pulled tight, revealing a smidgen more of the colorful ink.

Though I knew very little about him, I was drawn to him in some invisible tug of war. It was too early to consider Stockholm syndrome. Besides, I wasn't convinced this was truly a kidnapping even though I'd used that term.

No, this feeling wasn't new. The attraction began the night of the gathering. It was more than the untamed beauty of his handsome face and the secrets he kept contained in the ink under his clothes. In the unlikeliest of places and circumstances, I recalled the hardness of his body when he held me against him in my bedroom. As if it were more than a memory, my nipples hardened as my core twisted.

"It's the cool basement," I told myself.

While watching him held its own fascination, I wanted to see what he was seeing.

Was it about me?

About our formula? Our compound?

About my friends?

Finally, his green gaze came my way, staring as if he had heard my thoughts, as if I'd spoken them aloud.

"If I'm going to be here, I need a hair dryer?" It was the first thing I could think to say. A hair dryer wasn't a necessity, but in my overwhelmed state, it was better than blurting out that I found him insanely attractive in a unique, dangerous way.

"Make me a list." He stood as I followed his movement, taking in his height and breadth. Each step my direction was graceful yet powerful—a predator on the hunt.

Was his prey on the screen or standing here in yoga pants, a t-shirt, and no bra?

My top lip disappeared beneath my front teeth.

Kader came to a stop and leaned his weight on the plastic wall. "I'm not sure about a hair dryer though."

Tugging my lip free, I asked, "Why?"

"They make noise and use a lot of electricity. Remember, we're staying under the radar."

I pointed to his computer setup. "I'm sure that uses significant electricity."

"Not as much and it's more important than dry hair."

I didn't want to debate. "What are you doing over there?"

"Work. Research."

"I'm a scientist you know."

He nodded. "I'm aware."

"What I do isn't all in the lab. A big part is like that." I tilted my head toward his computers. "I am very good at research. I could use your computers and check some trails to see if I can figure out who wants to kill our research and development and why."

Kader shook his head. "I need to leave for a few hours. Grab a few water bottles. There's some fruit in the refrigerator if you want to take it to the bedroom."

My heart sank. The last place I wanted to be was back in that concrete box of a room. I stared his direction as we participated in a silent conversation, my expression saying I didn't want to go while his said I would. With a deep sigh, I went to the refrigerator and pulled out a bag of grapes and a water bottle. "You know what's not in that room?"

"My computers."

I stood and faced him. "A bathroom."

"Then use it first. I can't promise when I'll be back. Besides it's nearly eleven. You're usually asleep."

My initial instinct was to ask how he knew when I slept, but before I could, the first part of his statement brought my panic bubbling back to life. Laying the grapes and bottle on the table, I started to reach for him. My fingers brushed his sleeve.

His reaction was an immediate pulling away.

I stared up at the fire in his gaze.

"I'm sorry." I brought my hand back.

He didn't respond.

"I know, you said speak. I am trying. Touching is something I do."

He shook his head and took a step toward me, forcing me to raise my chin to meet his laser glare. "That rule is nonnegotiable.

I didn't want to fight about it. "I'll try."

"No, Laurel, there is no gray area."

"You've touched me."

His Adam's apple bobbed as he continued looking into my

eyes. The fire was still present though it had changed. Where my attempted touch ignited fire and fury, what burned now were the simmering hot coals of something deeper.

I couldn't help but wonder if *touching* applied only to my hands because at this moment, if he were six inches closer, his chest could brush against mine and my diamond-hard nipples would have the advantage that apparently my hands couldn't explore. I took a deep breath, yet contact was still too far away.

"Kader, what if something happened to you while you're out? This really isn't safe for me to be here alone."

"Nothing will happen to me."

"How do you know?"

"I know." He tilted his head to the table. "Now pick those up and take them to the room...unless you're waiting for me to put you over my shoulder."

With a quick look his direction, I picked up the bag of grapes and plastic bottle and stepping around him, I headed toward the bedroom. Coolness seeped up from the floor through my socks yet his body's heat radiated from a few steps behind me.

If I stopped quickly, would he too?

Once I reached the doorway, I spun toward him, coming to a stop with his wide chest before me. I looked up. The fire had died—extinguished or was it contained? I wasn't certain. "Where are you going to sleep?"

"I don't sleep."

"Everyone sleeps."

"The recliner out there is fine. Like I said, I'll be between you and that door."

I nodded and entered the room I'd said I wouldn't.

"I'll be back." It was the last thing he said.

That was all at least two hours ago. Now, I presumed the time was approaching one in the morning, yet I wasn't sleepy. I'd slept most of the day. It didn't help that I couldn't see the outside and had no way to verify the time of day or night myself.

That meant I had one choice.

Trust Kader.

While at times I thought I did, other times he frightened me. To be honest with myself, at this moment as I sat alone in the room that I'd said I wouldn't enter, everything frightened me. My mind was all over the place. One thought was the time of year. It was springtime.

What if it wasn't fire that destroyed the building above me but a tornado?

The only reason I'd entered the locked room willingly was because in the pit of my stomach, I believed that if I hadn't, Kader would have carried through with his threat, putting me over his shoulder.

The question I continued to ask myself was how much I trusted him.

Though he'd mentioned removing my shirt and examining the tracker when he was making his point, since our conversation and until he left, he'd essentially left me alone.

There wasn't a lock on the bathroom door. As I'd stripped

out of my clothes, I'd watched the knob, wondering if he'd try to enter. The entire time I was under the stinky water, I'd been prepared to tell him to leave.

Admittedly, by the time I dried myself and wrapped a towel around my body, I was disappointed that the knob never turned. It wasn't like I wanted anything from him. It was the memory of the intensity of his stare on my breasts as he secured the transmitter.

Russ and I had our thing. He could usually satisfy me. It wasn't like fireworks erupting on the Fourth of July. It was more like the refreshing release of a waterfall. From every indication, the feeling was mutual. Russ often seemed to find his own relief. Yet never had my heart beat erratically or my skin peppered under his gaze.

Perhaps that was what I wanted. In all this craziness, I'd wanted Kader to enter the bathroom and stare at me through the shower door with the same intensity he'd had in his eyes last night.

That was all.

Nothing else.

Maybe with everything that was happening, I longed to lose myself in that feeling—if only for a moment.

I had my suitcase, now on the floor in the bedroom, but there was nothing else.

Did Kader have my phone?

My purse?

If he did, he hadn't offered those to me. I could understand my phone, if I was to stay under the radar as he'd said.

However, there was nothing in my purse that would allow me to fly onto the radar.

Throwing back the blankets, I stood upon the concrete floor and walked the length of the room and back.

Four paces.

Turn around.

Four more steps.

If the concrete blocks were eight by sixteen inches, the standard size, this room was roughly ten by eight feet. Assuming the blocks were eight inches high, the walls went up nearly eleven feet. That seemed deeper than a normal basement. I didn't have one in my house, but the ceiling in my parents' was much lower.

Kader's questions and comments came back to me. He'd told me to dig deep and not sweep anything under the rug.

He'd said that the two men wanted information.

What had they wanted?

What would they have done to get it?

Why was the lab closed?

What about Stephanie?

Who would release information on the clinical trials?

All I could hope was that Kader would learn something.

What about Russell?

Why had he left me alone with those men?

My feet stopped walking.

How had Russ even known to be at my house?

I hadn't questioned it as it was happening, but now the timing of his arrival didn't make sense. Even if Russ had gotten a similar call, mine had only come minutes before. He couldn't have gotten to my house. And then I remembered, he hadn't gotten a call. He didn't know about mine until I told him.

Why did he show up at my house in the middle of the night?

And then why had he left me?

Kader said to look at the big picture, but quite honestly, there were too many small ones requiring my attention.

On the list of needed items he'd told me to make, I'd written laptop. The request wasn't even met with a verbal response. He took the pen and crossed it out.

After some debate, he agreed to pens, pencils, and paper.

It was antiquated, but it would help.

If this was all happening because of the formula, I wanted to write down everything I could remember. Lying back down on the bed, I stared at the ceiling's beams and the lone light bulb as the years of research and work floated around in my head.

Startled awake, I sat up and stared into the darkness.

LAUREL

When had I fallen asleep?

My hands searched the bed around me, patting the blankets and stretching my fingers, as my heart beat out of control.

Had I heard something or was it in my dream?

It had sounded like a roar or rumble, reverberating through the dark room.

Finding the remote, I hit the button to turn on the light above. My eyes blinked, adjusting to the brightness while at the same time, my ears strained, ready to hear the noise again. Scooting closer to the headboard, I pushed my unruly hair away from my face and stared toward the closed door. The anticipation of hearing it again had my senses on full alert.

What had I heard?

My mind searched for possibilities.

A big truck on the street above.

Thunder.

A lion.

Lifting the blankets that had fallen to my waist, I clenched them to my chin. It wasn't a lion, my reasoning told me that.

A tornado.

After all, this was spring in Indiana. My gaze darted up to the beams high above. I'd heard that a tornado sounded like a train. I couldn't be sure if that fit the description. Was the house above me being torn apart? From *The Wizard of Oz* to news videos, my mind filled with flying houses and pictures of destruction.

I gripped the edge of the blanket and returned my focus to the door. Under the covers, my flesh peppered with goose bumps as I silently waited for more.

The beat of my heart kept time.

Seconds.

A minute.

Nothing.

Lowering the blanket, I let out a long breath. Next was inhaling. Exhaling. The pattern continued until my pulse calmed.

"You're just on edge," I told myself.

I moved my gaze away from the door and took in the room as a whole. Nothing seemed different and yet I wondered if Kader had entered. I had no memory of turning off the light or falling asleep.

The lack of knowledge was wearing on me.

Moving to the edge of the bed, I threw back the covers. As my bare feet came to the concrete floor, I saw my yoga pants. The ones I'd worn last night. I scanned my attire.

I did recall taking those off as well as my socks and slipping into a long t-shirt.

Stepping over the discarded yoga pants, wearing only the t-shirt and my panties, I made my way to the door. If the noise was something dangerous, I needed to know.

Was Kader back?

I had no way of knowing.

Leaning my ear against the bedroom door, I held my breath and closed my eyes. The sound that had awakened me hadn't recurred. In reality, it was as if there was no sound at all.

My ears strained as I continued to listen to the nothingness.

Biting my lip, I reached for the doorknob. Twisting my wrist, it turned.

I wasn't ready to rejoice yet. Turning the knob had never been the problem. Even when it was locked, the knob turned. With my shoulder against the barrier, I pushed the door. To my relief, it moved outward. With the sound of my pulse thumping in my ears, I stepped into the hallway; my bare feet on the cool concrete sent chills down my limbs.

As I was about to turn back and put on the yoga pants, a new noise came into range.

Step by step, I followed the sound. I wasn't headed toward the large room but the other direction. Stopping outside the bathroom door, I listened as the shower's spray filled my ears.

The shower didn't explain the noise that had awakened me. However, it brought a whole new thought process to my mind. Kader was in the shower.

That meant...

Closing my eyes, I leaned my forehead against the cool wall beside the door.

I'd only seen Kader fully clothed. My mind swirled with the possibilities of what lay beyond the door. I imagined the sight of Kader behind the glass shower door, water flowing over his dark blond hair, over his wide shoulders, and down his powerful long legs.

All it would take was a turn of the knob to bring the image to life.

It wasn't his cock that dominated my thoughts although the thought of it hardening in my lower back made it high on the list. No, it was the man beneath the mask who I sought to find.

I longed to know what he kept hidden and the story his colorful ink would tell.

Who was he under the disguise he wore?

That wasn't literal. I didn't believe Kader wore a costume. His disguise was the way he hid his emotions. How even at the event when silencing Damien in front of a group of people, Kader showed no outward signs of stress. Calm in the face of pressure.

With two men—adversaries—on the main floor at my

house he wasn't nervous. Upstairs in my bedroom, he exuded strength and control.

There were a few times when his eyes momentarily darkened with desire, but it hadn't lasted long. Before I knew it, he had slipped the mask back in place.

What was he hiding?

The rush of water continued as my body reacted to the knowledge he was close and exposed. Under the light t-shirt, my nipples grew hard. I could tell myself it was the coolness of the basement, but the warming heat between my legs told the truth. In the middle of something dangerous, I was insanely attracted to the man behind the door.

And then another thought came to mind. He had unlocked the bedroom door.

Why?

Did he want the bathroom door's handle to move as I had earlier?

What would happen if I opened the door?

My imagination worked overtime as his words from before came back to me, their memory rumbling through me like the possible thunder I'd heard earlier. *"If you were on the auction block, I'd double the highest offer. I could have taken you the night of the gathering, against the wall or over one of those tables. I could have marked you as mine."*

Without conscious thought, my hand rested upon the doorknob while the other one made its way under the hem of my soft cotton shirt. The tips of my fingers skirted up over my warming skin. From my upper thighs I moved higher, no longer able to lie to myself.

My body wasn't reacting to the coolness of the basement. My reaction was due to the proximity of one man. Over my stomach I traced as my breathing deepened.

Closing my eyes, I created an image—Kader's muscular build covered in color.

The picture in my mind was beautiful and dangerous.

My hand moved higher as I gripped the knob tighter.

It wasn't like I had never gotten myself off before. It was that I don't recall ever needing it this badly, as if finding release was the only way I could go forward. Every nerve, voluntary and involuntary, sparked to life, sending off stimuli. My fingers climbed higher under my shirt.

My breasts grew heavy with need as I reached for one nipple and then the other. Tweaking each one, I repeated the move, harder and harder until I whimpered in both pleasure and agony.

The stimulation to my breasts sent bolts of lightning to my core.

I needed more.

Down my hand moved, between the valley of my breasts, and over my sensitized skin to the band of my panties. My breathing slowed until I wasn't certain it was occurring.

Through the door the water continued to fall.

A fleeting thought told me that this was crazy. If Kader were in the shower and my door was unlocked, that meant I could leave, gather my things and go. While that should have been my first thought, it was buried beneath the overpowering need I had to finish what I'd started.

Continuing my hold of the doorknob, I bent my knees, succumbing to the overwhelming primal yearning boiling within me. Crouching lower, I allowed my knees to spread farther apart. Forget over the top, I was going straight to where I needed relief. My fingertip brushed over the moist, soft cotton crotch of my panties as another moan escaped my lips.

Biting my lip, I slid two fingers under the edge.

"Oh," I whispered as I found the extent of my own desire.

My orgasm was there waiting for me, stronger than any I'd had recently with Russ or than I'd ever given to myself. I was on the edge and it wasn't because of the way I rubbed my clit or the tightening of my internal walls.

It was the colorful picture in my mind.

Beautiful, powerful, and dangerous.

So close.

In my mind it was him, Kader's hands upon my skin, teasing my clit, and kneading my breasts.

The release was in sight as I crouched lower.

The doorknob moved in my grasp—the latch clicking.

"What the fuck?" Kader's growl came from the other side of the door.

Shit.

No longer brought on by desire, my pulse raced with fear. I'd wanted to see him, to open the door. Yet I hadn't. Not intentionally. Letting go of the doorknob, I stood. Without looking back, I ran to the bedroom and closed the door behind me.

Why hadn't I heard the water stop?

The answer was as obvious as my still-slick-fingers.

Maybe if I climbed in bed, I could pretend I was asleep.

That was my plan.

Pulling back the covers as I fumbled with the remote, I scooted onto the bed and turned off the light. He couldn't see me in the dark. I burrowed into the sheet lifting my long hair away from my now damp neck. I only needed a few minutes and my breathing would be normal. He'd never know what I'd done.

As time passed, I became more confident in my plan.

Yes. This would work.

I'd never had sex in public. While the thought was intriguing, the reality of being caught was too much of a deterrent.

Then why had I done what I'd done in the hallway where Kader could hear?

Had I wanted to be caught?

No.

I wanted a reprieve from what was happening. I'd wanted relief.

My breathing began to slow as I turned, curling on my side.

"It's probably the middle of the night. You can make yourself go back to sleep," I said to myself.

The conjured vision of Kader under the shower faded as I worked to steady my breathing as well as my heart rate.

I was almost there, almost convinced that I hadn't been caught.

The door to the bedroom opened with enough force that it bounced off the wall.

I couldn't help myself from looking.

Would he be naked?

Covered with a towel?

My head lifted from the pillow.

"Laurel."

LAUREL

*T*he timbre of his voice rippled through the darkness.

Since a moment ago when I was in the hallway, the lights had all been turned out. From the degree of darkness surrounding Kader, I believed that included the light in the bathroom. He was again a dark silhouette surrounded by gray.

With my elbows supporting me, I stayed silent as he took a step forward.

As if extinguishing a candle, the little bit of light around him disappeared. The clicking of the latch and the thud of the door against the frame told me the door was now closed.

He wasn't trying to be quiet. He was here to make a statement.

Butterflies turned to bats in my stomach as the room filled with silence.

What would he say?

What would he do?

Though I was surrounded with darkness, I knew he was here, possibly close enough to touch.

The aura that surrounded him, that of power and control, vibrated through the air. The musty scent of the basement room faded, giving way to the fresh scent of recently cleaned skin and shampoo.

The warmth I'd felt earlier between my legs came rushing back. It may be wrong to want him, but that didn't stop my desire.

"Kader." I replied, my voice sounding strange even to my own ears.

Was the strange tone due to shame for what I'd done or perhaps frustration by my unmet need?

Every nerve in my body knew he had come closer.

Why had he not spoken?

"I-I'm sorry. I didn't realize you were in the bathroom."

Closer still.

It wasn't that I could hear or see him move. I knew he moved.

I gasped as the blanket above me was ripped away, exposing me. And yet nothing was exposed in the darkness.

His deep tenor registered within me. "What the hell did you think you were doing?"

"I-I just needed—" Instinctively I reached out to find his proximity. For a millisecond my fingertips met his solid chest, hard muscle with an uneven surface. He backed away too fast to fully describe what I'd felt.

"I've told you..." His commanding tone echoed from the cement walls. "...do not touch me."

Pulling my hand back, I laid my head on the pillow. "Will you touch me?"

The echo of his command ceased to exist. My question hung in the air.

Time stood still.

And then he spoke. "Lift your arms over your head."

"Kader..."

The rest of my statement was lost as strong, powerful hands seized my wrists.

Before I could argue or say a word, his lips captured mine, bruising and controlling. The taste of his kiss was lost in the brute force of its delivery. I was right. I was no match for this man. I couldn't fight him off if I wanted to. The truth was that at this moment, I didn't want to.

Fighting him was the furthest thing from my mind as I lifted my head, pushing toward him.

Kader was a mystery in all ways, from his appearance at the gathering to the golden flecks in his green eyes and the colorful tattoos he kept hidden. And yet I was drawn toward him. The more ruthless his kiss became, the more I wanted.

It was as if he were a black hole, and such as with the cosmic body, I was inexplicably pulled toward him. My need was for more than this current entanglement. The bats that had been flying about my tummy with fear or anticipation when he'd caught me had settled into a spiral flight pattern, twisting my core tighter and tighter. There was no logical explanation for my desire. And as the room filled with primal sounds it was clear that when it came to me, Kader exceeded the normal gravitational pull.

The more he took, the more I wanted to give.

My breath, my safety, my body—my destiny—they were all in his hands.

The mattress sagged as warmth covered my legs. Long legs straddled my body, my thighs trapped by their powerful muscles. His chest hovered over mine. I pushed upward, trying to raise my upper body, wanting to feel him covering me, flattening my breasts as my nipples hardened under his weight.

As if knowing my plan, Kader pulled my wrists higher, painfully, elongating my arms so that I was captive to his hold. Through it all, his mouth sought more than I'd ever before given, unapologetically claiming what had been mine.

Despite the positioning, he was a master at his craft, allowing me just enough space to breathe while maintaining complete control. The pressure of his thighs was like a vise holding me in place, and yet he leaned closer.

Oh God.

I gasped.

He was naked.

The hardness of his cock prodded my stomach. The light cotton of my t-shirt was no shield against the pressure of the steel rod pushing against me.

Mint toothpaste teased my taste buds as his tongue demanded entrance.

Like his cock against my tummy, his delivery wasn't sweet or gentle. It was pure domination executed with perfection. Our tongues didn't dance as they might in a tender first kiss. They fought. He was an explorer and I was the land he planned to pillage. He'd said something about marking me. My mind was too full of him to remember exactly, yet as we battled, it was clear that I was being marked.

Coming up for air, I pulled back, pushing my head into the pillow as my hips bucked under his weight. It wasn't like I could move them much. However, by his guttural groan, he felt it. My hands tingled from his grasp of my wrists.

"Please..." I managed to say.

"What do you want, Laurel?"

I could ask for many things. I could request information to shed light on the situation. I could ask about my friends. Yet at the moment, those issues didn't pop to mind.

"I want you to take me." I sucked in a breath. Before he spoke again, I added, "And please let me touch you."

His face came down to mine. His nose touching mine as the shake of his head brushed it back and forth. "I fucking want to take you. To make you mine." The pressure on my wrists loosened. The hold was there, yet blood was once again free to circulate. "But I can't."

He could. The rock-hard cock prodding my stomach told me he could.

"What?" Disappointment settled over me like a cloud.

Kader lifted his weight to his knees and pulled me by my wrists until my hands collided with the headboard. "I'll let go of your wrists if you promise to hold the metal rungs. Don't let go, Laurel. Hold on tight."

"Why? You just said..."

I didn't finish speaking. Kader was prying open each of my fingers and placing them on the rungs.

"I said I can't make you mine," he clarified. "That doesn't mean I don't want to see you come."

See? How could either of us see?

Before I could respond, his body shifted and lips touched my skin.

Hot and cold.

Fire and ice.

That was what he was doing to me.

Kisses and nips rained over my neck and collarbone like fire laying waste to every inch traveled. As soon as he moved, the places he'd been froze over, wanting and needing more of his attention.

"I've been wanting to do this," he murmured.

I screamed out, my voice echoing through the room. My reaction was brought on as much by surprise as by pain. His teeth came down, taunting my nipples, one and then the other, sometimes hard, other times softer. There was no discernible pattern. Expecting his next move was outside my current reasoning. Whatever his mouth did, wherever it went, sent surges of electricity to my now-saturated core.

His lips moved lower while his large hands held my hips in place.

The dark room filled with sounds, moans of pleasure and whimpers of surprise.

It was as his teeth snagged the edge of my panties that my skin pebbled and the small hairs on my limbs stood to attention. Inch by inch, his bite was pulling them down while his hands continued to hold me in place. As the undergarment moved lower, his coarse facial hair abraded my sensitive skin.

"Oh God..."

"Don't let go."

It was a good thing he'd reminded me. I'd almost forgotten about the headboard as my panties came down to my ankles and disappeared in the darkness.

"Fu-uu-c-k."

I wasn't sure how he'd done it, taken one word and elongated it until it reverberated through not just the room but through me. Yet he had.

"O-oh, damn..." Words were flowing, yet I wasn't in control of their pronunciation or meaning. The first lick of his tongue on my core and I was gone. The climax I'd denied myself earlier ripped through me. A jolt of electricity. Lightning in the sky.

Fast and unexpected, it was an F-5 tornado and once it was done, I was left in ruins.

Kader had said not to let go, but that was exactly what happened.

Not with my hands.

One lick and the destructive sensation snaked through me. My entire body bucked off the bed, only to be recaptured by his grasp. I panted for air as my essence flooded my core.

And yet he didn't stop.

Kader pushed my knees higher and lowered his face to where it had just been.

"I'm...I don't know if I can..." My sentences were incomplete, as incoherent as my thoughts.

"Fuck that. I've just started."

I didn't think it was possible, not after the way I'd reacted. *How could he just be only starting?*

My fingers blanched as I tightened my grip. More licks. His tongue was as determined to please my core as it had been to enter my mouth. Higher and higher he played me, teasing and taunting, licking and biting. He took me higher and let me slide back. The process was exhausting. Perspiration coated my skin. My untethered hair was glued to my neck. I'd run a marathon and yet not moved from this bed.

As if granting me a reprieve, his grasp shifted and his thumb stroked my clit. The blackness of the room was shattered as fireworks exploded, their sound muffled by the noises and disjointed words I could no longer hold back.

Through it all, I may have begged for it to end while simultaneously demanding it to continue. My memory was unclear.

The grand finale ripped through me like a life-altering earthquake.

That was what Kader was: every trick of Mother Nature

was at his fingertips. Never before had anyone shattered me with the force of thunder and wind while also causing the earth to move.

Muscles lost all tension. My hands dropped from the headboard as my knees fell apart, and my lungs gasped for breath.

The mattress again moved.

The warmth disappeared.

I was free to move at will, yet my energy was depleted.

In the darkness, I was once again alone.

The realization hit me as I rested in the aftershocks of what I'd just experienced.

Without a word he opened the door.

I wanted to call out, to say something, to thank him or yell at him for doing what he did and leaving. I wasn't really sure what I wanted; however, as the sound of sliding locks broke the now-heated air, I knew the answer didn't matter.

Without taking me, without having sex, Kader marked me.

One day, I could walk away from what was happening.

I could walk away from him.

Yet like his colorful hidden designs, his mark of me would forever be present.

KADER

$\mathcal{M}$y entire nude body trembled uncharacteristically as I stalked away from Laurel and down the concrete hallway toward the bathroom. The rigidity of my dick ached as it bobbed with each step. I didn't stop until I was in the bathroom with the door closed.

Throwing open the shower door, I prepared to do what I had done during my earlier shower, what I'd done after I checked on Laurel. I entered the bedroom as soon as I got back to the safe house. Her transmitter had gone silent. No verbal transmission. No heartbeat. Once I'd seen that on my phone, I'd rushed back.

With the light still on in the bedroom, I found her sleeping in a fucking t-shirt, one so thin I could see the dark circles around her nipples. Her body was curled on its side in sleep. Her ass was mostly covered by white panties lined with lace.

No fucking thong or black sexy lingerie.

Like her bra had, the panties screamed innocence.

I had studied her for weeks. I knew she wasn't a virgin. I knew about her arrangement with Cartwright. If I dug more, I'd probably find more lovers in her past. That didn't bother me. It wasn't my fucking business. Besides, innocence wasn't about virginity. It was about her state of mind.

Innocence was her cloak such as danger was mine.

Seeing her lie there, there was no doubt; I wanted her, to take her, to make her mine in every way. The need was painful, strong, and irrational. I was a man in control yet when faced with a sleeping woman, I was out of control.

Not any sleeping woman—Laurel Carlson.

Standing silently over the bed, the scene came alive vividly in my mind—too fucking real. My fingers recalled the feel of her breasts as I'd placed the transmitter. I'd told her that the next time I took off her shirt I wanted to do more. More was in my mind's eye, a daydream so real my pulse hastened and dick grew accordingly.

I pulled her from her slumber, her ass in my hands, until her feet hit the floor, leaving her body facedown on the mattress.

With my weight over her back, I whispered in her ear, my warm breath trailing over her skin. "Doc, you're almost safe. The pieces are starting to come together."

"Thank you."

I reached for the hem of her shirt.

Willingly she lifted her arms as I stripped the transparent mate-rial from her soft curves. Before she could stand or turn, I placed one hand in the small of her back. "Don't move."

Her body trembled under my touch, yet she obeyed. With the skill of a craftsman, I peeled her panties from her hips to her ankles.

The ass I had seen covered in white satin and lace was in front of me, bare. I ran my hand over her softness as small whimpers filled the room. Wedging my foot between her feet I spread her legs. Light reflected on the visible essence on her upper thighs. Widening her stance, her pink pussy quivered.

I couldn't resist touching her first. Like liquid satin, her cum allowed my fingers to plunge into her warmth.

"Oh!" she called out.

Leaning over her, I moved her arms to the sides of her head. "Don't let go."

Her fingers clawed at the blankets as I lowered the zipper on my jeans. With a flick of the button, my hard dick sprang free.

"I'm going to fuck you."

"Yes," she whispered. "Make it all go away."

Grabbing her hips, I thrust into her.

Her shout bounced off the walls as I pushed in again.

So fucking wet and tight.

The scene didn't happen.

The blood on my hands shielded her as I forced myself to walk away. I turned off the light, leaving her untouched in the dark.

Why the fuck hadn't I locked her door?

I hadn't locked the door because I didn't think of it. I was busy convincing my dick to forget her. Laurel Carlson had a hold on me that I couldn't control.

I controlled everything.

Earlier tonight I'd stepped under the shower's spray and taken care of what I could. The make-believe scene replayed behind my closed eyes. There was no honor in what I did with my dick in my grasp as my balls drew tighter and tighter.

In my mind I was back in the bedroom.

My relief came with a roar I couldn't restrain as stream after stream of seed coated the shower. Finally my head fell to the plastic stall. It had taken me a few minutes to gather my thoughts. Laurel in my mind was better than every professional I'd ever encountered physically.

That was earlier, before the fucking doorknob moved.

And now I was back, my throbbing dick again in need of relief.

This time I didn't step inside the shower. With the glass door open, one hand gripped the metal surrounding the door with enough force to bend it, I again reached for my dick.

The grip on the metal was gentle compared to the one surrounding my dick. I was done with this shit. *I* was in control, not some part of my body. Faster and faster my hand moved, pulling and pushing. It wasn't relief I sought. I'd already done that. This time it was punishment—my sentence for allowing Laurel to change my plans.

Faster yet I moved, my balls growing tight and the skin reddening with the abuse.

This wasn't like it would be inside Laurel. My lips opened at the pain I inflicted.

"Fuck!"

More seed spewed as my hands gripped the shower's entrance. This time it wasn't relief that snaked down my spine but determination.

Turning on the water, I watched as the evidence of my weakness washed down the drain.

Turning away, my neck straightened and jaw clenched as I stared in the small mirror over the sink. My fingers blanched as I gripped the edge of the porcelain. When I met my own gaze, I was grateful that the mirror wasn't larger. Nevertheless, it was enough.

"You're not a man," I said aloud. "A man has more than one name. They took that from you. You're a job, an assignment. You don't deserve a woman like her. Fucking get this job done and over."

Letting go of the sink, I scanned between my reflection and my own body, looking down at my chest and over at my arms. They'd told me one time how many surgeries I'd had. I stopped listening. They were never fully forthcoming with the information.

An explosion.

Fire.

Unfathomable pain.

Time disappeared.

When I walked away from the devil, I was no longer the man I'd been.

Looking back at the mirror, I recalled what I'd been told. The best plastic surgeons had done what they could do. Their emphasis had been on my face and hands.

I lifted one hand, splaying my fingers and turning it over.

There was very little evidence that there had been burned flesh. My hands were no more scarred than those of the ranch hands in Montana. They were workingman's hands.

My face.

My gaze went back to the mirror.

I had little recollection of my appearance—or my life—before my date in hell. It didn't matter. The being in the mirror now was who I was today. I supposed I was thankful for some of the things that happened during those months. I was grateful for the surgeons who had given me a face. If it were as wrinkled and coarse as the skin of my body, I would be captive to the shadows. Because of those men and women, the shadows were my choice.

I ran my hand over my arm.

Grafts and cadaver skin.

Necessary to retain my bodily fluids.

Thicker and stronger than normal derma, the scars were my reminders that once I'd had a life.

Fire was a powerful tool. It could wipe out ten thousand acres and disintegrate a life.

I couldn't return to the one I had before, not because I desired this life. I couldn't return because like the forests lost to wildfires, my life before was gone. They'd saved my body at the cost of my mind.

The full-body tattoos took a trusted artist years to complete.

Visually, the colors disguised the scars.

They didn't take them away.

They were still there.

The reflection in the mirror was why I would never allow Laurel to get close to me. Why I never allowed anyone to touch me. Even the whores I hired knew my rule. It was and would always be nonnegotiable. It was also why I locked her door. I wouldn't take the chance of her walking in here on me.

Taking a deep breath, I turned away from the mirror, gathered my clothes from the floor, and made my way down the hall to dress. Once I was covered, I'd open her door.

I refused to dwell on what happened a few minutes ago in that bedroom. Like my past life, I'd remove it from my memory. Laurel would rightly be repulsed by the man beneath the clothes. I wouldn't give her the chance.

I'd gotten my taste of her. It was more than I deserved.

It was time to tell her what I'd learned and move on.

LAUREL

*D*ressed again in my yoga pants with a bra under a fresh t-shirt, I paced the now-lit bedroom—waiting. While my mind wanted to think about what had just happened with Kader, those thoughts created a pathway taking me back to why I was here.

The formula.

The compound.

Our current trials.

The men at my house.

The break-in that wasn't.

Stephanie, Russell, and Eric.

Before...we'd...before I woke, Kader had left the safe house.

I wanted answers.

My steps stilled as I turned toward the door, propelled by

the sounds coming from the other side. The sound of sliding and clicking of locks was magnified as I crossed my arms over my still-tender breasts. Taking a deep breath, I squared my shoulders and waited as the door moved outward.

It wasn't that I expected roses, cuddling, or a candlelight dinner after what we'd done. It was that I didn't expect nothing.

Absolutely nothing.

As the door moved I could see that the hallway was also illuminated, showcasing the man filling the doorway. His customary boots and jeans were in place. The black thermal from before was replaced by a dark blue long-sleeved shirt, unbuttoned near the top with a gray t-shirt beneath covering the ink I'd seen before. The fresh scent of his showered skin was replaced by the rich cologne he sometimes wore.

Similar to Kader's clothes or cologne, I'd started to realize his expression was also something he wore. Rarely did it change. Sometimes when we talked, the edge of a smile would break through his stoic expression. I would like to think it had been different—realer—earlier.

I wouldn't know.

The room had been too dark.

Dark could describe the expression he wore now, the same dark mask he displayed most of the time.

"Bathroom is free," he said. "I have breakfast down the hall."

Fisting my hands at my side, my nostrils flared as I let out an exaggerated breath. "Really?"

"Fruit and bagels." And with that he turned toward the large room.

I rushed to the hallway, my steps determined. Pulling the door toward me, I called, "Hey."

Kader turned on his heel. "What?"

"Are you kidding me? We need to talk about...well, a lot of shit."

His expression remained unmoving. "Fine, Laurel. We'll talk. I will do even better."

"What's better?" I asked with my fist now on my hip.

"I'll respect your privacy and not get off outside the bathroom while you're in there."

My eyes grew wide. I wanted to deny what I'd done, but I couldn't. "For your information, I didn't get off, as you said, outside the bathroom."

He took a step toward me. "No, you didn't, but you were fucking close." The cords of his neck popped to life. "I heard you. I fucking heard you before the doorknob moved."

"So what was that?" I pointed toward the bedroom. "Are you a full-service kidnapper? Save me from fake police and make sure I have an orgasm?"

A strained smile came to his lips. "At your service, Doc. Thank me by doing what you need to do and eating. I have work to do."

"And that's all you're going to say about it?"

His smile was gone. "Nothing more to say. You wanted it. I gave it to you. If it's this fucking big of a deal, next time do it yourself."

I spun toward the bathroom. "You're un-fucking-believable." With each step a lump grew bigger in my throat, my chest grew heavy, and the hallway blurred.

Oh, hell no.

I was not crying because of him.

I didn't even know him.

He sure as hell didn't deserve my tears.

I was almost to the bathroom when Kader's hand came down on my shoulder, stopping my retreat. "Turn around."

As his fingers splayed, I turned my gaze to his hand. Powerful and strong, his hands appeared capable of honest hard work. I imagined him chopping wood, not pushing a pencil or sitting before a computer. Yet they'd also brought me pleasure.

After what he'd said, I didn't want to look at him. His fingers gently squeezed.

What alternative did I have?

Sniffing away my emotion, I took a deep breath and turned toward him. I lifted my chin until his green-eyed stare was bearing down on me.

"Laurel, you're in a dangerous game right now. That...what happened...can't happen again. You're under stress. I'm not going to apologize to you."

I swallowed. "I wasn't expecting an apology."

"What were you expecting?"

"Hell, I don't know, Kader. Something. Words. Talking."

His head shook. "Sorry, Doc. That's not me." He tilted his head toward the bedroom. "That's not me either. That's why it can't and won't happen again. I have a job to do. I'm going to do it and get the hell away from here."

I reached toward him. As if having a sixth sense, just as quickly, he took a step back.

"Sorry," I mumbled.

His eyes went from my hand, floating in the air awkwardly and then back to me.

"Kader, you are right." I lowered my hand as heat filled my cheeks. "I'm scared and alone here. I don't know who to trust. I know that I'm only a job to you. I get that. I guess I let my imagination get out of hand. I find you intriguing, and yes, you're right about what was happening—what I was doing. I'm not proud of that. I'm also not like that..." I pointed to the bedroom. "...either. I don't do..." I recalled the earth-shattering orgasms as more heat filled not only my cheeks but also radiated down my neck. My head shook. "I can honestly say that nothing like that has ever happened before.

"I guess I simply wanted both of us to acknowledge that it did happen."

"What good does that do?"

"It will help us move on."

His chiseled jaw clenched as he nodded. "It happened. I acknowledge. I've moved on."

I didn't respond.

"Now hurry," he said. "There are things that happened outside of this basement that you should know."

My fingers clenched and unclenched as I tugged my upper lip between my teeth. "Do I want to know?"

He shrugged. "Dangerous games aren't about wanting. We all want. It's about digging and learning the truth. It's not all pretty. But I think you've lived in the dark about a lot for too long."

"I don't understand how you can learn things about my work that I don't know."

"I see the world as it is."

My breasts moved as I let out a breath. "Okay. Give me a few minutes." The queasiness in my stomach replaced any hunger I might have had.

"I'll get breakfast on the table."

Maybe Kader wasn't the type of man who cuddled, but there was something about his desire to feed me and even inform me that felt genuine.

"I'm not very hungry."

He didn't have to reply. I could see the slight change in his eyes.

"But a bagel does sound good," I said, forcing a smile. "I should probably eat."

As I turned to enter the bathroom his hand again landed on my shoulder.

I was on the verge of mentioning the inequality of this touching rule, but when I looked up at him my lips came together. Something had changed, and yet if I were pressed to name it, I'd be unable.

"You were...I just don't want you to think I didn't...I'm not the person for you. I do things. It's my work—who I am, but none of that matters. How I live and what I do, I accept responsibility. I live by my choices. What that means is that I'm not a person for anyone. I'm not apologizing for what I did because I'm not sorry. I'm letting you know that if I were someone else, I'd sure as hell do it again."

My lips curled upward as warmth again filled my cheeks.

What was that?

Not an apology and yet it made me feel better.

"I don't know you well enough to know what kind of person you are," I said, "but I do know that you're trying to help me. I also know that what we did was...good." My smile grew. "Better than good."

"Now we move on," he said.

"Yes."

Entering the bathroom, I closed the door. With a sigh, my body fell against the unlockable barrier as my eyes closed. I would probably relive the scene in the dark for the rest of my life. And that was what I needed to concentrate on—having a rest of my life.

Finishing our research.

Moving on.

Opening my eyes, I squared my shoulders and turned to the small mirror above the sink. A scoff escaped my lips.

No wonder Kader wanted to move on.

My hair had a serious case of sex-mess. I wasn't wearing makeup and yet my lips were red and swollen. Despite it all, the dark circles from before had disappeared. Even under the horrendous lighting, my complexion looked improved. Perhaps sleeping most of yesterday had its perks.

As I took care of business, washed my face, brushed my teeth, and brushed out my hair, I'd occasionally glance toward the doorknob. I would no longer hope for or worry about it opening. He didn't need to either.

Kader was right. Shit was happening that was too dangerous. That was where our focus needed to be.

Opening the door, I walked toward the big room with a new purpose.

There on the table was a bagel, cream cheese, and a plastic bowl of fruit. Next to it was also a tall white cup that made me smile. "Coffee," I said, more in praise than observation.

Kader was behind the plastic wall.

"Are you going to eat?" I asked.

"I ate." A hint of a smile cracked his facade. "Coffee is the way you ordered it at the coffee shop. But it's probably cold. I...well...got sidetracked."

"Thank you," I said, sitting and removing the plastic lid. I wasn't certain if my gratitude was for the coffee and food or for him getting sidetracked. I supposed it could be all-encompassing.

"Finish eating and I have some things to show you over here."

"You're going to let me see?"

His smile disappeared. "No, Laurel. I'm going to insist that you see. Your ass isn't leaving this chair until you know the truth."

LAUREL

Kader's words churned in my stomach, mixing with the cold coffee and bites of bagel. The more I tried to eat, the more nauseous I became. By the time I stood, less than half the bagel was gone and I'd simply plucked the blueberries from the mixed fruit.

With each step, the cool liquid sloshed against the sides of the cup. It wasn't due to my steps but because my entire body was now trembling. My fingertips were white, as if the already-cool basement had dropped twenty degrees.

With my thumping heart pushing my circulation like a drum in my ears, I stopped at the edge of the wall. It was the boundary he'd given me the day before, one I wished still existed.

Kader's broad shoulders eclipsed the back of his chair. His lips were set in a straight line surrounded by his unshaved facial hair. I tried not to think about the coarseness or how it felt on my sensitive skin. His hair was again bound behind his head. The changing illumination coming from the screens reflected in his green stare. His long fingers ruled the keyboard as they had my body.

There were no clues in his stony expression of what he wanted me to know, to see. In two steps it would be visible. I would be able to see what he was seeing.

My feet didn't move. Perhaps the cement had softened and re-hardened. That would explain why my socks were now glued to the floor.

It wasn't the floor. It was me. I was scared to learn. If Kader was right and I hadn't been seeing the world as it truly was, perhaps I wanted to stay uninformed.

Taking a deep breath, I wrapped both hands around the cool coffee.

This wasn't me.

I was a scientist, a researcher.

Over my life I'd faced untold numbers of disappointments and setbacks. That was part of the process. No one succeeded the first time. That's what I would tell my graduate students, the ones whose work I facilitated individually or in small groups. I would ask them to describe their results. In the beginning, I'd be met with the response that the results didn't matter. They didn't validate the hypothesis.

Why?

That was my question.

I wasn't forcing them to wallow in their failure. That

wasn't my intent. I wanted them to find success in their perceived failure because that was when real understanding occurred.

Many great discoveries were uncovered in discarded data.

"Dr. Carlson, it didn't prove my theory."

"What did it prove?"

It took a while, but over time, the same students would come to me, wide-eyed and excited.

"Did you validate the results?" I would ask.

"No. Let me show you what I did find..."

"Laurel." Kader's deep voice pulled me from my thoughts back to the reality of what was on his screens.

"What are you going to show me?"

The chair rolled back as he stood. "Come sit down."

My circulation slowed, falling toward my feet. The room began to spin.

"Laurel?"

Strong arms surrounded me as the cup fell from my grasp to the concrete below. Cold coffee splattered. At the same time, I was lifted from the ground. Kader was speaking. His words and sentences vibrated from him to me, yet they held no meaning. I was floating in a tunnel and the walls were closing in.

"Laurel, what the fuck?"

When my eyes opened I was lying on the sofa with a cool washcloth over my forehead.

There was no disorientation. I knew where I was and what I needed to do.

Sitting up, I laid the washcloth down and shakily stood.

This time when I made it to the wall, I feigned a smile. "I think you saved my ass again."

His granite expression cracked as one side of his lips moved upward. "You're a fucking full-time job."

"What happened?"

"I'm no doctor, but I would say you fainted."

A soft chuckle rolled from my lips. "Astute diagnosis, Dr. Kader."

"You need to do this."

I nodded. "I know. I'm ready."

Kader did something on his keyboard and stood. Catching the chair with one hand, he motioned for me to sit. Settling into the large vinyl chair, I felt the warmth of where he'd been. When I looked up, the screens before me were black.

Kader went to the other side of the plastic and brought back one of the chairs from the table. Spinning it around, he straddled the back, scooting next to me.

"It's taken me weeks to learn this much," he began. "I thought about what you said. You know your research better than anyone. I would assume even better than Dr. Cartwright. If we're going to crack this, we should work together."

I let out a long breath. "You want my help?"

Why had I expected pictures of death and destruction?

"With parts of it."

"Okay," I said, the queasiness waning.

"I think we should start here." He leaned forward, his arm brushing mine.

My gaze shot to him, expecting a reprimand about touching. He was focused on what was happening on the screen.

"You need to see the email I told you about."

Kader hit more keys and clicked the mouse. His movements happened too fast for me to follow a pattern or learn his pass codes. And then it appeared.

I leaned forward processing the words.

The clinical trials are underway...

By the time I finished reading the entirety of the email, my head was shaking vigorously. "This can't be real." I turned to Kader. "It can't be. No!"

"Quiet."

I stood so fast the chair shot back, hitting another table. None of it was registering.

"Listen," I said hastily. "You want my help? Here it is. That email is fake." I pointed to the screen. "It isn't real. It can't be. We don't have those results yet. It would take a broader group of recipients to come to those conclusions. Our sample size is too small."

"I guarantee this email is real. Are you sure the information within it isn't accurate?"

"Am I sure?" I was walking and rubbing the back of my neck. My mouth was dry, making me wish I hadn't spilled my coffee. "Of course, I'm sure. I know what we have and what we need to still do. I've lived and breathed this research for years. No one except me and Russ could be sure."

"Settle down. This could change my theory."

My steps became faster. Back and forth I paced. What had been too cold minutes ago was now too warm. "Did you turn up the heat?"

"What?" Kader asked, turning away from the computer.

He'd gone to something else. It looked like surveillance videos.

I pulled at the neck of my t-shirt. "The heat? I'm burning up." It was then I spotted the door in the corner, the one he'd told me to stay away from. Without thinking, I changed my direction. "I need air."

Apparently, the way to escape a kidnapping did not include announcing your intentions to leave.

Before I could reach the door or even reach out to turn the knob, Kader was in front of it, a mountain of a man separating me from the outside. I met his stare head-on. "Get out of my way."

"No way, Doc. You're not leaving."

My palms slapped my thighs as I spun. "This is a concrete cage. I can't...I need to find out who wrote that and why."

"That's exactly my plan. To me, the why is obvious. You're a genius. Shouldn't you see it?"

I shook my head. "What does IQ have to do with anything?"

"Come over here and sit down." Kader reached for my hand and tugged me toward the computers.

Wistfully, I turned back, watching the outside door get farther away with each step.

With a sigh, I sat again in the soft chair and lifted my hair from my neck.

Kader gave me a sideways look. "I'll get you a bottle of water if you swear to keep your ass right where it is and that you won't spill it all over my computers."

My lips pursed and twisted to the side.

"No, Laurel. Words."

"I could lie to you."

"You won't," he said matter-of-factly.

"Fine. I will stay here but I can't promise the spilling part. I'm known for my clumsiness..." My thoughts went to the way Russ teased me about that over the years. "...and there's no guarantee."

He pointed to where I was seated. "I mean it. Don't move."

"You could work on not being so bossy," I called through the wall, watching as he retrieved a bottle from the small refrigerator.

Coming back, he handed me the bottle and took the seat beside me. "Give it to me after you take a drink." He tilted his head. "I believe you. I'm not taking any chances with my equipment."

The cap had already been loosened. The cool water soothed my dry mouth and refreshed my throat. "Thank you." I secured the lid and handed it back.

After setting it on the floor, Kader took a deep breath, the inhalation straining the seams of his shirt. "I assumed the email was written or at least dictated by Cartwright," Kader said, his cadence slow and deliberate. He was ready to get back to business.

What?

"No." I gripped the arms of the chair. "Russell wouldn't do that."

"This email is soliciting buyers. I'm not talking about investors. Whoever wrote this recognizes the value of your compound and all of its potential. Based on the email's contents and other observations, I thought it was pointing to Cartwright." Before I could respond, he went on, "But if the information isn't valid, if it's inaccurate, that begs the question, why?"

"Why?"

"Are you two the only ones who would know that this information is inaccurate or misleading?" Kader asked.

I leaned back and gave it some thought. "No. Eric would know. Truly with how closely she works with me, probably Stephanie too." I continued to stare at the screen that again held the email. "We have had various assistants and there's the medical staff at the clinical facility." I shook my head. "No, the email is too close to accurate to be written by one of those people."

I turned his way. While I had been looking at the screen, Kader was watching me. There was something in his expression, something I didn't recognize. "Do you know something you're not telling me?"

"I know a lot I'm not telling you."

My grip of the chair arms tightened as I wiggled on the large seat, unable to sit still. "Will you tell me?"

He lifted his chin toward the email. "After this. I want to talk this out first. If I tell you, you'll be distracted."

"But will you——?"

Kader's hand covered my knee, his fingers splaying as he gave it a squeeze. The warmth of his palm radiated through the material. My gaze went from his hand to his green eyes. The illumination from the large screens brought the gold flecks to life.

"Yes."

"Okay then," I conceded as the heat of his touch disappeared. "I suppose there are more candidates than I would like."

"That makes me wonder if the inaccuracies were intentional, to take the heat away from those who would know better, or was it accidental because the author of the email doesn't have all the information."

I shook my head. "That doesn't narrow it down."

Kader leaned forward on the back of the small wooden chair. "I placed trackers in the wallets of the men who were at your house."

"Did it lead anywhere?"

He moved the mouse again. A new screen came up. It was a map of Indianapolis and surrounding areas. There were pin-looking icons as well as streets covered with different colors.

"This is tracking them. So far they've stayed away from the university."

I pointed to one icon. "Why is this one red?"

"They've been there multiple times."

"Did you check it out?"

His expression was unmoving. "Yes."

I began to stand, again unable to stay seated.

"Sit down. I don't want you fainting again."

Considering my rapid pulse, it was good advice. "What did you find?"

"Who."

My skin heated. "Who?"

"Stephanie never made it to her chaperoned trip to the university." He took a breath. "I've gone through the surveillance. She never returned to the university labs or offices alone or with fake policemen. She was last seen leaving on Monday night."

Heaviness filled my chest. "What does that mean? Did you find her? Did you go to her place?"

LAUREL

*K*ader let out a long breath before shaking his head.

"What are you saying?"

"Your assistant is gone, as in missing. However, I have reason to believe she was at that location." He pointed to the red icon. "I found her badge, the one to access the fifth floor. I haven't determined what that means. Cartwright also hasn't been seen. I have his place wired for surveillance. It's like he vanished into thin air after leaving your house."

I lay my head against the back of the big chair and turned my gaze to the man beside me. "I can't believe any of this."

"Laurel, I'm telling you the truth—"

"No. That wasn't what I meant. I can't believe this is *all* happening, not that it isn't true or is. I'm not sure. There's just *so* much." I emphasized the all-encompassing words, my thoughts going back to life before last Friday. My family came to mind. "Oh God. I've been too self-centered the last few days. Do you...my family? When you and I spoke the first time, I got the feeling you were threatening them."

"I haven't left Indianapolis."

So that's where we still are. I figured as much; however, he'd never said so.

"I need to call them," I said.

His lips came together as if he wanted to respond but was holding it back.

"Or could you send someone to check on them?" Moisture came to my eyes. "Please. This is my family. My sister is divorced and lives with my niece. Her daughter is only five years old." I looked around. "If I had my phone I could show you pictures."

Kader stood, backing away from the wooden chair as I waited for his response. "Laurel, the goal in the bidding war is about the formula and resulting compound. It's not about your family."

Standing, I took a step toward him. "And you know that for sure?"

He nodded. "I mentioned your family because as I said, what I do isn't legal. I wanted to leverage them in your decision to name a price—a price to step away, to sell out. I thought it would work. I've done my own research on you. I've seen your pictures. Those clouds where you and others store all their shit from pictures to tax returns are not difficult to access."

"Then if you accessed it, someone else could too. Can't you call someone to check on them?"

His lips came together and nostrils flared. "I work alone. It's how I do my job."

Collapsing back into the chair, the weight of it *all* came down, pushing the breath from my lungs. My mind filled with what I'd been told. "Kader, Russ and I had a plan to keep our information—our parts of the research and results safe. Did it work? Have you been able to get to it?"

"I haven't and I've been trying."

Guilt snaked through my being as I contemplated my next move. I could tell Kader about the flash drive and how Russ had a similar one. Or I could tell him what we'd done—how we'd made one exception.

I wasn't proud of it. It went against our plan from the beginning.

It happened a few months ago, when the talk about investors first began. Russ and I had been together talking—more than talking. We'd agreed to not fully trust anyone beyond the two of us. After all, the formula and resulting compound was our baby.

It almost felt that way.

Neither of us had children, but together we'd birthed a compound, one that we believed had unlimited potential.

Wasn't that the same as giving birth to a child?

My sister, Ally, believed anything was possible for her daughter, Haley. I remembered visiting her in the hospital after she gave birth. The pink, wrinkly baby in her arms was tiny and cooing. She was completely dependent on Ally and her husband. And yet they spoke of her future, what they wanted for her, and what she could become.

That was the way Russ and I felt about our creation.

We'd been spending the night at my house.

A few months ago~

I'd rolled to my side, facing away from the man who had just been with me—inside me. It wasn't because I didn't want to see him. I was simply tired, and despite the sheets twisted around our naked bodies, we weren't the cuddle-after type of couple.

Someday I'd want that, I thought.

Right now, this was fine—good.

My relationship with Russ was simply different.

The cool winter wind blew the panes of my windows as my lids grew heavy. To my surprise the warmth of his body spooned behind me as his arms snaked around my waist.

"Laurel, do you ever worry about what could be done with it?" he asked.

He was talking about our compound. It was our life. That was why it was nice to sometimes go beyond the working relationship. There wasn't another woman who he could talk to about it or another man for me. It was our connection.

Our limited clinical trials were giving us some mixed data.

Yet we'd seen some success. Dosage and frequency of doses were some of the issues yet to be determined. A blanket dose for everyone seemed impossible. There were too many variables.

"Worry?" I said, sounding more like a question. "I like to concentrate on the good it can do." I turned in his grasp until we were nose-to-nose. With only the light coming from around the blinds, I was struck by the way he was staring at me, the sincerity in his gaze. This was why our partnership worked. Stripped bare of the pretenses of the university, we were honest with one another. "What are you thinking?"

He shrugged before landing a quick kiss on my nose. "I guess I worry."

"We all worry, Russ. Eric is stressed about funding. The results from the clinical trials are less conclusive than we'd like. But this subset is small. I believe we can learn from these results before going to the larger trial."

"It's more than that. I..." He didn't finish his sentence. Instead, he turned, staring up at the ceiling.

His dark hair was messed and his cheeks sported their normal five o'clock shadow. Yet his profile was the same I saw almost every day at work. Calculating, concentrating, and dedicated.

Under the blankets, I reached for his hand, entwining our fingers together. "We have our plan. No one will get all the data. Not without us. Dr. Oaks can't pressure Eric into anything without the consent and knowledge of both of us."

No longer sleepy, we spent the next hour or more, our

heads on our pillows, talking about scenarios, possibilities, and solutions. While we trusted the others who worked with and around our project—they'd all signed confidentiality statements—it was clear that our level of faith wasn't as high with them as it was with one another.

Finally, Russ moved from the bed.

I watched as he walked to the fireplace and removed the stone, the one that usually hid my flash drive. Now the space behind the stone contained both of our flash drives. When he turned back to me, his expression was set. I'd known him long enough to know he thought what he'd proposed was right.

I scooted up to the headboard and brought the blankets over my breasts. While I was covered, he was not. Sitting on the edge of the mattress, Russ handed me both flash drives.

"Are you sure?" I asked.

He nodded. "In reality it will be outdated after tomorrow." He scoffed. "I mean, today."

He was right. It was now well past midnight.

I looked down at the flash drives in the palm of my hand. I didn't want to think about alternative uses of our work. That was why I concentrated on the positive. Seeing the two flash drives and knowing their contents, a sense of pride washed through me. "We did this," I said with a smile.

"We did."

I closed my fingers around them. "We don't have a safe place to combine them, one that can't be traced."

"You're right. I'll get an external hard drive."

I nodded. "Where should we keep it?"

"Not at the university. We can't risk anyone else getting it."

"Okay," I agreed, "if it's small enough it can go in there." I tilted my head toward the fireplace. "I have a safe, but if someone were looking, that's where they'd look. Only you and I know about the fireplace."

"I'll get one that fits. And then tonight after work, I'll come back here with you..."

I listened, wondering if it was a good idea to deviate from our original plan while at the same time, feeling the same sense of urgency to protect our work—our baby.

"...and we'll continue to maintain our own data. Then every couple of months, we'll update what's on the external hard drive."

"Just one external hard drive?" I asked.

"Just one, Laurel. The more we have, the more we're setting ourselves up for someone else getting their hands on it."

Present~

"Laurel, look at this." Kader's voice pulled me from the memory, bringing me back to the reality of the musty basement. My gaze went to the screen. The map from earlier was gone. We were now looking at surveillance footage.

The screen was subdivided, each square containing

surveillance feed from various locations. Most I recognized—my house, Russ's apartment, our offices, and the lab. There were others I didn't.

"Where is that?" I asked as I pointed.

"That's Dr. Olsen's home. The cameras rotate from the outside to a few different locations within."

I shook my head. "How did you do this?" My lips came together for a moment as I contemplated what we were seeing. "This feels wrong. It's like we're invading his space or stalking him."

"I have to know where each of the main players is or try to anyway."

The locations could very well be still pictures. There wasn't any movement.

And then there was.

"Shit." Kader's deep voice growled, pointing at the screen.

Shock and relief simultaneously washed over me. "Oh my God, that's Russ. Who...?"

LAUREL

*T*he relief I'd felt washed away as quickly as it came as the feeds from my house disappeared, the square going fuzzy and then black—first the one of my side door and then the one from within my kitchen. However, not before we saw Russ enter the kitchen, his key to my house in his hand and another figure behind him.

"Was there someone with him?" I asked, knowing I'd been concentrating on Russ. "Did it look like...?" My lower lip disappeared behind my front teeth as I stared from the screen to Kader. "I thought I saw someone behind him? Who would he let in my house and why?"

"Fuck." Kader pushed closer to the keyboard and mouse. Each command he sent went without response.

"Why would we lose the feed?"

"Two options. Your internet or the cameras were disabled. If it's the internet, I should get it to come back with 5G."

It wasn't coming back.

Kader continued to type. The other squares remained active.

"That isn't good. I didn't get a good look at the other person." My fingers twitched, wanting to help, as if I could do more than Kader. I stood, wrapping my arms around my midsection as Kader continued his flurry of keystrokes. "How could anyone know about your cameras?" I asked aloud.

Taking a deep breath, Kader stood, scooting his chair over the floor and turned my direction. Offering me his hand, he said, "Come with me."

"Yes, let's go there." I placed my hand in his. "We can find out what's going on and why he disappeared and who that person was and..." Excitement returned to my voice as I continued my sentence. "...maybe he knows about Stephanie and Eric too."

"That's not happening."

Kader tugged me toward the hallway.

"Excuse me?" I stilled my steps and pulled my hand from his grasp. "If you think you're going to put me in that room and go to my house without me, you're wrong."

His green gaze sent a chill down my spine. The tightening of his jaw combined with the cords coming to life in his neck said that he meant business. "I'm not wrong. Laurel, you have three seconds or the over-the-shoulder option is in play."

"Kader, listen to me. I trust Russ. I know you don't. You

said that yourself. But I do."

"One."

"Stop it," I said, taking another step away. "You said I was part of your job. I need to tell you some things if you really plan to help me save my research."

"Two."

I took another step back. "If you touch me, I'll scream."

"You're wasting time. He wasn't alone. Whether he's trustworthy or not, I have a gut feeling. That's how I work."

"You said you wanted my help." I spun toward the computers and pointed. "We were working together." I thought of the flash drive. "Come in the bedroom with me." I walked past him, spinning as I neared the doorway. "Please. This is important. Do not shut the door. I trust you. Don't disappoint me."

It was almost imperceptible, yet I saw it; Kader gave me a quick nod. It wasn't a guarantee, but I didn't have many options.

Turning on the remote for the overhead light, I rushed to the suitcase still in the corner of the room and searched the lining. The small pocket was designed to hold important items. Most women probably used it for jewelry or money. In my small pocket was the flash drive I'd taken from my house.

With it secured in my hand, I stood and turned.

Kader was standing as he had the first evening when I'd awakened. His hand was on the doorjamb and his massive shoulders nearly filled the frame. His green stare wasn't looking at me, but at what I was willing to share.

For a moment my steps stilled.

I knew virtually nothing about this man.

Stephanie's assessment came back—she said he gave her the creeps.

And yet I was drawn to him in a way I couldn't describe. The pull was the same as the first time I'd seen him. It was more than his build and beautifully handsome face. It was the unique aura that radiated about him.

Power.

Determination.

Danger.

The quantum electrodynamics model described the interaction of positive and negative ions. Depending upon their proximity to one another and their charge, their attraction was inevitable. The model didn't explain *why*, only that this phenomenon existed.

That was the way it was with me to Kader—an unstoppable attraction.

I didn't need to understand *why* it was there, only that it existed.

Though part of me said that I shouldn't, I trusted him. It was a realization that I didn't want to fight.

I stood before him and opened my hand.

"It's incomplete," he replied.

My head began to shake. "How do you know that?"

"You were unconscious for nearly ten hours."

I took a step back. "And you...you...? It was in my pocket. You touched me?"

"You didn't notice the black card was gone?"

My head moved from side to side. "I...I guess I didn't." There had been too much. My gaze met his, wanting an answer to my first question. "My pocket?"

"I reached into your pocket. I didn't touch you..." He appeared to stifle a micro change to his expression. "...until later. This conversation is wasting time." Stepping back, his other hand reached for the door.

Immediately, I stepped forward, blocking its path. "Russ has one just like it with the other half of the data. You said your employer wants to stop our research. You also said there's a bidding war. You can protect the research if you have both drives."

The door continued to move.

"Kader, there's something at my house, something only Russ and I know about."

The door stopped.

"Where? I searched your house."

"Take me with you and I'll show you."

"Tell me," he demanded.

"That will take longer."

"Fuck. Get your shoes. We're leaving now."

When I entered the large room wearing my shoes and coat, Kader was wearing a black hooded sweatshirt and placing a gun in the small of his back. I stilled, wondering again about the danger. "Is that necessary?"

Instead of answering, he pointed to the kitchen table. "You can't wear your coat. It's recognizable. Put that on. It will keep you warm and more importantly, it will keep your identity hidden."

"Why do we want to do that?"

"Hurry."

The sweatshirt strewn onto the table was identical to the one he had on. When I lifted it, the bottom hem came to my thighs. "I can't wear this. I'll swim in it."

He didn't respond.

Pulling it over my head, his scent surrounded me, the aroma of cologne combined with the fragrance of his skin after his shower. I pushed my hands into the sleeves. With the hood over my head and my black yoga pants, he was probably right. No one would recognize me.

After the giant hoodie was in place, Kader began his instructions. "Don't make a sound. Not after we go up the stairs, not until we're away from here."

I nodded.

Removing the gun from his back waistband, he held it at his side as he slid open a lock and opened the doorway at the far end of the basement. "Stay right behind me."

Since what we were doing was out of my realm of knowledge, I didn't question, doing exactly as he said. The stairwell was narrow and tall. Gripping the railing, I followed. The wooden steps creaked under his weight and again under mine. I'd thought to ask if they were safe, but pressed my lips together, remembering the order to stay quiet.

My pulse sped up to an unhealthy level as his long fingers spun the tumblers of a padlock with speed and proficiency.

Placing the lock in his pocket, he again positioned his gun, and slowly opened the door to the world above the basement.

"Oh..." I gagged.

The sound I'd made was quickly met with a silencing green-eyed laser gaze.

Lifting the neck of the sweatshirt, I covered my nose and mouth, creating a mask to stop the offending odor from infiltrating my senses. Blowing out, I sought the masculine scent of the material, trying to ward off the stench of the room we'd entered.

As he closed and padlocked the door to the basement, I couldn't believe my eyes. The small rooms were in a state of disarray. Holes like Swiss cheese created openings within what had been walls. Clutter with debris filled the corners. Step by step we dodged piles of trash and animal droppings, as well as items that had long ago been abandoned. The windows were covered with boards. It was as if the house had been host to the homeless population of Indianapolis.

Kader led me through what had at one time been a kitchen. The cabinets were missing their doors and the appliances stripped away. One more doorway and we were within a garage, face-to-face with a beat-up Chevrolet truck.

He walked to the passenger side and opened the door and then a smaller one. Behind the front bench seat, he pulled down two small seats from the back wall, reminding me of jump seats on airplanes. "Get in and lie down over the seats," he whispered. "You can't be visible."

LAUREL

"Are you serious? That isn't safe."

"You're right, it's not," Kader said, tilting his head toward the area behind the bench seat.

Shaking my head, I did as he said, crawling forward. The space was designed for children or very small people. It definitely wasn't designed for a grown woman and not one in a supine position.

As I tried to find a way where the seatbelts wouldn't prod me, the door closed near my feet. A few seconds later Kader was inside the cab, and the rumble of a garage door opening filled my ears.

How could there be a working garage door in this hovel?

The truck roared to life, vibrating the seats. Slowly, he backed out of the garage and into the world. From my position, I could only see upward. The darkening dusk sky showed through the back window. Being in the basement had warped my sense of time.

My lack of acknowledgment hadn't stopped the clocks. Another day was about gone.

"Stay down," he said. "Tell me what's at your house, what I didn't find."

"We—Russ and I—had an agreement. We would each maintain a portion of the data. That way it was only when we were together that it could be accessed."

I took a deep breath. Even with the distant scent of exhaust, the air was better than within the main floor of the house we'd just passed through. I recalled the stench and debris. "Where are we staying? That house…"

"It's disgusting."

"Why?"

"No one will bother it," Kader said. "While people like you carry on your life, neighborhoods like this are forgotten. They're invisible. Over time, I've found areas like that work best when I want to also be invisible. It's like this truck. There are so many like it around here, no one notices. If we were driving around in a Bentley or even a Tesla, people would take note."

"The basement…it's not great, but it's so much better."

"Yeah, I did some work to it and installed the garage door too. The garage opens to the back of the house. The backyard is overgrown with trees and bushes keeping it hidden. I didn't plan on having a guest, so it's not up to your standards."

I sighed, remembering Kader at the gathering, his expensive suit and shoes. "I'm not certain it's up to your standards either."

"Tell me about what's at your house."

"A few months ago," I went on with my story, "Russ and I decided to back up all of the data together. We planned to update it periodically. There were things happening that had us both uneasy. We never backed it up again, so the data is a bit incomplete compared to our individual flash drives."

"Where is it?"

"There's a fireplace in my bedroom. It's stone. On the far side, away from the hallway, there's a loose stone. It's lower than eye level and not very noticeable. We'd dug out some of the mortar behind the loose stone and created a hiding place. Once the stone is situated back in place, it's secure. I figured it was even fire resistant."

"You have a safe."

His observation made the small hairs on my neck stand up. Instead of asking how he knew, I asked, "Did you look in it?" Maybe it was my way of coming to terms, as much as I could, with the knowledge that Kader had invaded my space.

"Yes."

"That's why I liked the fireplace. It was less obvious."

Kader hummed. "I'm impressed." Before I could respond, he continued, "If that was Cartwright's mission, he's probably long gone by now."

"I just..." I searched for the right way to ask the question on my mind. "...did you offer him the same deal...a price?"

"He wasn't my assignment. You are."

"I don't understand."

From my position I could see his broad shoulders and the back of his head.

"I didn't make him the same offer." Kader shrugged. "That doesn't mean that my employer or someone else didn't hire another person for Cartwright or Olsen."

"Or Stephanie," I said, hopeful that they too—all of them—had someone keeping them safe.

"It's not like there is a list of job postings. That's not how this works."

"I can't see," I said as the sky grew darker and streetlights came to life. "Nothing but up. Where are we?"

"We're almost there. I'm going to drive by your house first and see what's happening. I'd suspect he's gone. Even so, someone could be watching your house. I don't want to take the chance of someone seeing you."

The rumble of the tires over the roads was the only sound as the truck slowed, stopped, and moved again. My thoughts were consumed with Russell Cartwright. I told him I didn't have a price.

Had he?

He'd said that he didn't, but did something change?

"Do you think this has to do with Sinclair Pharmaceuticals?" I asked, breaking the silence.

"I think it's a player or it's being played. Like I said, the bidding is beyond anything you can imagine. We're talking multimillions."

"The continued research will be equally as costly."

"From my understanding, none of this is aimed at continuing your research."

"That doesn't make sense. Once the compound is perfected and available for sale, the revenue will surpass the bids. Hell, it will surpass all the costs."

"The bids haven't stopped. They're growing higher. The only car in your driveway is yours."

"Why does anyone want to stop it?" I asked.

"I don't ask questions. I'm hired, do a job, and move on." The truck slowed and came to a stop. "Wait until I open the back door." When the door opened, he whispered, "Put the hood up, stay close. We're a block away. The plan is to go through a few yards and avoid being seen."

Standing, I assessed our location. We were in a driveway that curved behind a house not too far from my home. I'd driven by this place, but I didn't know who lived here. "Won't these people see us?"

"They're out of town for the winter."

"How do you know that?"

"I know everything about you, including your neighbors' schedules. Pretending to be them, I sent an email to their close neighbors telling them about some repairs that would be going on in their absence."

He reached for my hand, led me down an embankment, and into a tree line. We were mostly hidden by the shrubbery.

"I've been parking there off and on for the last few weeks," he said. "This neighborhood is different than the location of the safe house. In a place like this, nothing is invisible. Around here, people care or are simply nosy. The repairman ruse is a simple explanation for the presence of the truck. It lessens curiosity."

Kader tugged my hand, bringing us to a stop at the edge of my yard. "Wait here. If Cartwright or someone else disabled my cameras, they could have installed new ones. If that's the case, you can't be seen entering."

"It's my house."

"Trust me."

The more twisted my life became, the more I did trust Kader.

Nodding, I pulled the sleeves of his sweatshirt over my hands and wrapped my arms around my midsection. From my vantage point I could watch from afar. I wasn't certain what he had in his hand, but whatever it was, he was aiming it at the doors and windows. Slowly, he made his way around the perimeter until he disappeared around the other side of my house.

I could run.

The thought came and then more.

If there was a price on my head, did I want to be alone?

I could bang on Mrs. Beeson's door. She'd help me.

Then again, what if helping me put her in danger?

I couldn't do that.

And then the internal debate came to a halt.

Kader was no longer outside my house but within my kitchen.

The lights were off, but I had come to know his silhouette.

This was it: decision time.

Run to Mrs. Beeson's or follow him inside?

I crouched down. Taking a deep breath, I ran hunched over, the hood covering most of my face. This was like a scene from a police drama. Only this time, I was the bad guy, breaking and entering my own house.

I wasn't certain that was possible.

Easing around the side of the house, I scanned all directions. The weather was still cool enough to keep people inside. Holding my breath, I reached for the handle of the outer door. My grip tightened to keep it from blowing out of my hand. I pulled. The storm door opened easily. I turned the knob to the kitchen. With a push it also opened.

The familiar scents and sights welcomed me. It was home.

Why couldn't Kader make sure I was safe here?

Now that I was here, I didn't want to leave.

During my run, the hood had fallen. I pulled it back over my head and as quietly as possible, closed the doors behind me. For a moment, I stood still and scanned my kitchen. It seemed to appear as it had been when I left.

Were there cameras?

I wanted to call out to Kader, but the fear of being overheard kept me silent.

With each step, my overactive nervous system transmitted impulses, quickening my circulation and numbing my extremities. My breathing shallowed and body stilled as my foot landed on the fourth step of my staircase.

Shit.

The squeak echoed through the house.

Had someone heard that?

Was anyone here besides Kader?

Why hadn't I stepped over it?

Obviously, my mind was too filled with everything, with Russ and the external hard drive. I waited. The air around me remained silent except for the sound of my furnace blowing warm air through the registers.

When I reached the top of the stairs, Kader appeared from my bedroom. Even in the mostly dark hallway, I saw his intensity in the tightening of his jaw.

Seizing my shoulders, he gripped tighter than ever before. His words were a growl. "I told you to wait."

"I saw that you were in here. Is the external—?"

"Laurel, we're leaving *now*."

"No, wait. You don't know which stone. I'll show you."

His grip intensified as he stepped my direction, blocking my entry. "Now."

Perhaps it was my need to see if the backup external hard drive was gone. Maybe it was pent-up frustration at the twisted situation or his continual stream of orders. With the help of the oversized sweatshirt and a quick twist, I freed myself from his grasp. I didn't have far to travel. One step, maybe two as I made it to my bedroom's entry.

My hand came to my mouth as the gut-wrenching scream poured from my throat. "No!"

LAUREL

a monumental force surrounded me, pushing me away while simultaneously blocking my view.

The stench of urine and something else unfamiliar permeated the air.

The lunch I'd eaten hours ago while sitting at the computers bubbled in my stomach, threatening to make its way up my esophagus. Kader twisted me, turning my gaze away and yet I'd seen.

The scene would never be unseen.

Russ lying lifeless on my bedroom floor.

Dark red liquid pooled around his face, soaking into the wooden floor.

His eyelids half-open and half-shut, as if he was staring blankly toward the bed, under the bed. The bed where we'd made love.

Was that what it had been?

His lips were parted and pale.

Had he tried to speak or call out?

Was it to me?

"How?" My cry was muffled by Kader's hold of me against his chest.

"Gunshot."

I remembered Kader's gun. He had it in the basement. He'd taken it with us. I hadn't heard a shot, but I didn't know anything about guns. On television they had silencers.

My legs regained strength. I pulled away, backing into the hallway.

"Laurel."

"No," I screamed as my hands balled into fists. In less than a second, I lunged forward, pounding, hitting, and punching against his solid chest. "Why? How could you? I told you I trusted him."

My tirade was short-lived. Kader's strong arms again engulfed me, capturing my flailing fists, and securing my arms at my sides. Again I was held in place, my body pressed against the hard muscles of the chest I'd just attacked.

"I found him. I didn't kill him."

His explanation faded into the foul air as he led me down the stairs. The familiar living room—my entire house—was always and forever changed.

How could I go on?

What could I do?

Words didn't form. Sentences were out of the question.

Even my hearing was affected.

The rooms filled with a buzz.

Maybe only I heard it because while Kader's arm was still around me, his voice rumbled in the distance. With each step my legs grew weak.

When we reached the final stair, I fell from his grasp, my body going limp. It was as if I'd turned to liquid, flowing from his hold and puddling onto the living room floor.

Russ had been the one shot, yet the pain from his demise consumed me. "I-I..." Sobs resonated from my chest. "No." I repeated the one word over and over as my head vigorously shook. "This can't be happening. We had a rain check."

Kader crouched beside me, his massive body supported on his toes as he leaned forward on his haunches. His timbre was slow and his tone low. "We need to get out of here."

My head was still shaking, the swish of my own circulation thundering in my ears. "No. We have to call the police. He was murdered." Saying the words made it real. I didn't want it to be real.

"Laurel, you can't be at a crime scene. I need to get you to the safe house."

"I can't leave him."

"You have to leave. There's nothing you can do for him."

It was then that I remembered why we'd come. I looked up, seeing something different in Kader's gaze. I couldn't assess the change. While that was what I did for a living, my mind was beyond the ability to decipher. "What about the external hard drive?" I asked.

"The stone was on the floor."

It was?

I hadn't seen it.

I hadn't seen anything but Russ.

"The space you created was empty," Kader went on, "nothing but a thin layer of mortar dust."

I imagined what he described. The dust accumulated regularly from removing and replacing the stone.

"Who was with him?" I asked. "On the surveillance, before it cut out, there was another person."

Kader reached for my hand and helped me stand. "I'll find out."

Though he was now leading me toward the door and we were in the kitchen, my gaze continued to look back to the living room. In my mind's eye I saw further. I saw Russell, my partner, my lover, my friend.

I imagined Russ sitting on the sofa with his ankle over his knee or at the kitchen table with a cup of coffee. That would never happen again.

He was gone.

If asked, I couldn't recall if I'd walked back to the truck or flown. Maybe I'd been carried. However it occurred, I was once again lying across the uncomfortable back seats as I'd done on the way to my house. Everything was a blur. And through it all, my thoughts were consumed with the gruesome images. With each turn or stop as we traveled the streets of Indianapolis, the victims in my mind changed.

My parents.

My sister.

My niece.

Eric.

Stephanie.

I pulled Kader's sweatshirt around me tighter, drawing my knees up until I was fully covered. The hood was over my head and yet I couldn't escape my thoughts or what I'd seen.

Everyone sees images of death. It's impossible not to.

They're everywhere: in movies, television shows, and video games. Our minds accepted those because we knew they were fiction. We expected them. The same was true in books. While the images weren't visual, they were nonetheless vividly created by words. However, they also weren't real.

Reality was more gruesome: news programs and crime documentaries, for instance. Those images were different. They weren't fictitious characters. They were actual people.

I scrunched my nose at the memory of the smell in my bedroom. I understood the physiology. A no-longer-living body often expelled its bodily fluids. My heart ached for Russ. The idea of anyone else seeing him in that state added to my anguish.

As the truck moved, my body continued to quake with uncontrollable sobs. Tears and snot puddled on the vinyl seat below me. I didn't care. Its presence barely registered.

There were only three things on my mind.

Russell was gone.

Our research was gone.

Eric and Stephanie were missing.

Wiping my face with the long sleeve, I took a breath and then another. While it didn't stop the pounding in my head, with time it slowed the tears.

"Kader?" My voice cracked with misery.

"We're almost there, Laurel."

"I thought you said it was me."

"What was you?" he asked.

"You said there was a price on *my* head. Why is Russ...?" I gasped for breath as another sob interrupted my question.

"I didn't know about him. To be honest, I didn't trust him. I thought he was selling you out, at the very least to Sinclair. As I've said, I was hired for *you* and the research."

I inhaled. "We need to find Eric. I don't want...and Stephanie..." My nostrils flared as I worked to fill my lungs. "I don't want anyone else hurt because of our...*my* research." Classifying what we'd created as solely mine constricted something in my chest. The pain wasn't metaphoric. Like the vision of Russ on my bedroom floor, it was authentic.

I drew my hands up to my chest and applied pressure to my breastbone, concerned that if I didn't physically hold it in place, my heart would leap from my body. The resulting gaping hole would leave me in the same state as Russ.

My now-swollen eyes closed.

Just as quickly they opened.

Would I ever be able to close them without seeing Russ?

I didn't know the answer to that.

LAUREL

*S*leepwalking.

That was the sensation as I climbed out of the truck and Kader led me through the litter and debris. Nothing registered. Not even the smell, which in itself was a miracle. I waited as he removed the padlock.

"Do you put that on when I'm here alone?"

"Yes."

"Then why lock the bedroom door?"

"This lock keeps anyone who might break in from getting downstairs. The bedroom lock keeps you downstairs."

I didn't respond.

I paused on the steps as he fastened the same lock on the inside of the door.

When he turned my way, he said, "Same thing. I'm not

anxious to shoot some trespasser simply because they were looking for a warm place to sleep."

Because of the position I'd been in while lying in the back seat of the truck, there was no way for me to be sure exactly where in the Indianapolis area he'd brought me. But from the look of the first level, I was certain I didn't want anyone but Kader coming down the stairs.

As I pushed open the door to the large room, a strange sense of safety settled over me.

I doubted it was more than my mind's overwhelming need to find a reprieve in the devastation that was now my life. I scanned the room. We were in the eye of the storm. That was what this was. The world beyond this concrete set of rooms was falling apart under the devastating category-five winds, and we were safe behind our storm shutters.

Still wearing Kader's sweatshirt, I collapsed onto the tattered sofa. My eyes closed as my chin fell to my chest. The faint tap of Kader's steps on the concrete created a soothing rhythm, allowing me to concentrate on it and not what I'd seen.

The steps came to a stop before me. "Laurel."

When I looked up, his hand was before me, palm up.

"Come with me."

"Where?" I asked as I began to stand.

"We can't leave Cartwright in your house."

I pulled back my hand and pushed myself against the sofa. "No, Kader. I can't go back. I-I..." The image came back as my eyes filled with tears. "...I won't."

Again his hand was before me. "Come with me to the bedroom. You're not going. I am. I can have it all cleaned up in a matter of a few hours and I'll be back."

My head was shaking. "What? How do you do that? The blood...my floor."

"Laurel, the sooner I go, the sooner I'll be back."

"I don't want to be here alone. Please, not in the bedroom." My gaze went around the larger room, beyond the plastic wall. "I won't touch your computers. I...I know the door is locked upstairs, and I don't want to go up there and have anyone find me. I promise." Desperation filled my plea.

Kader turned toward the table, lifting a water bottle and a small green tablet. "Take this. It will help you sleep. When you wake, I'll be back."

"Please, Kader, don't leave me alone."

"Take the pill. I'll stay with you until you're asleep. The cleanup has to occur tonight."

Wearily, I reached for the pill. "What is it?"

"Something to help you sleep."

"You'll stay until I'm asleep and you promise you'll be back when I wake?"

"Doc, you know how sleeping pills work. You had a bottle in your medicine cabinet."

I inspected the small round tablet in my hand. The medication I'd been prescribed was oval and white. "This isn't from my house."

"Come with me," he said again.

"I need to use the bathroom first, especially if you're going to be gone."

"Take the pill."

"I will, when I get to the room."

A million thoughts bombarded my mind as I made my way to the bathroom.

Was he right?

Would rest be good for me or would it be riddled with dreams—with nightmares?

Wasn't that what I was now living—a nightmare?

The bedcovers were pulled back, and the water bottle and pill were on a sideways-turned box when I entered the bedroom. Apparently the quantity of furniture within the room was growing, not the quality, considering a turned box was my new bedside stand. Sitting, I kicked off my shoes and reached for the bottle. My eyes closed as a new tear trickled down my cheek.

"Laurel." The pad of his thumb wiped away the moisture as his palm cradled my chin, bringing my gaze to his. "I don't want to leave you either."

"Then don't."

"If the police find him in your house and you're later found safe, you could be a suspect."

I shook my head. "No one who knows us...knew us," I corrected, "would say that. Russell and I were..." I didn't finish the sentence. I wasn't ready to use past tense.

"The big picture. That's what I told you to see. You're not. You see this from your perspective. We don't know who that person was who entered your house with Cartwright. We don't know what arrangement they had and why Cartwright would take him to the external hard drive. Maybe you found out that he'd given away the drive and you shot him."

"You know that's not true."

"I do. I can't help you in court. I can help you now."

I looked from Kader to the tablet and back. "I need a reprieve." Lifting the pill, I placed it on my tongue and removing the lid from the bottle, took a drink of water. "Don't leave yet."

Letting out a long breath, I lay my head down on the pillow. Above me the single light bulb glistened as never before. I blinked my eyes in rapid succession. The colorful display grew stronger. Prisms like rainbows danced over the concrete blocks.

"It's so pretty," I said. It was as the bed began to float that I called out to him. "Kader."

My cheeks rose at the sight of him surrounded by the bright colors.

"Laurel..."

My head tilted to the side as I scanned him up and down. "Are those colors coming from you?"

"What colors?"

His tattoos.

I'd only seen small glimpses.

I wanted to see more, but the words were no longer forming.

KADER

*R*ed swirled in the water at the bottom of the shower as the spray washed evidence of Russell Cartwright's demise from my body. The clothes I'd worn were bagged, ready to be incinerated.

Laurel's house was cleaned beyond perfection.

The shitty part about doing that was that I'd also erased any evidence of Cartwright's killer.

Whoever the man shown briefly on the surveillance was, he knew about the external hard drive. What he must not have known about was the part Laurel told me, about the individual flash drives. Cartwright's had been in his pocket.

What did that mean?

Why had he given up the external hard drive and not the up-to-date flash drive?

Had she been right in trusting him?

Did he hold back information on purpose?

Holding the plastic side of the shower, I lowered my face, letting the warm spray fall over my head, saturating my hair. If only the water could clear my thoughts as well as it was cleaning my body.

Laurel was still asleep.

I'd checked on her as soon as I'd returned.

She had reacted too quickly to the sleeping pill, strangely and incoherently. I waited, monitoring her breathing and heart rate before I left. I hadn't royally fucked this job to have her die from an overdose of one pill.

I didn't know if her trust had been misplaced in Cartwright or if he too were a victim. One thing was clear. She was too trusting of others.

After all, she trusted me.

With both of the flash drives, I could end this assignment tonight.

My head shook.

What the fuck was it about her?

Had I known her before?

No, if I had, she'd know me.

If I didn't recognize myself, could it be possible she didn't either?

I was grasping at invisible straws.

She was a feeling I couldn't shake; like no one else, she'd gotten under my skin.

The best thing would be to finish the job and move on.

As I dried my skin, my thoughts filled with Laurel and her ability to look at me—see me—talk with me. It was more than that. She made me want to converse. There was an inexplicable need to protect her even though I knew it was wrong.

My breathing deepened as my thoughts turned to the moment before she fell asleep in the other room. It wasn't only my lungs that took notice—my dick did too.

I scoffed at the memory. Laurel probably wouldn't remember the things she'd said or done after taking the pill.

I turned to my reflection, my grip threatening to crack the porcelain sink.

Before she'd gone unconscious, Laurel asked to see my colors as her small hands reached for the buttons of my shirt. She wasn't herself under the influence of the one pill. Nevertheless, her barely coherent babbling and requests revealed the truth of Laurel Carlson—the more I tried to hide, the more she saw.

In the mirror, I scanned the colorful swirls, wondering for not the first time, why I'd chosen them. It was difficult to have meaningful tattoos when there was nothing meaningful left in my memory. They told me it was the trauma of the explosion, my mind's defense. They said the past would one day return, or it wouldn't.

It hadn't.

Turning my shoulders, I found the army medallion on one shoulder, surrounded and hidden by other shapes and colors. On the other shoulder was the Airborne Special Forces insignia. They were both hidden, like one of those kids' games where they try to find the hidden pictures. On my stomach, the flowing lines had inadvertently created swirling cursive letters, ones that I could read if I looked down, making them upside down from another perspective.

The artist had apologized profusely, saying it was a mistake. He offered to add more decoys. I refused, agreeing only for him to add a Y. I had no idea who Missy was or if she had meant something to me. All I knew was that when my gaze found the name amongst the other colors, there was a tightening within my chest with a sense of loss I couldn't quite grasp.

It didn't matter that I hadn't planned on having a name on my skin. It was there.

I didn't need to see to know that on my back there were chess pieces camouflaged with more colors.

I wasn't certain why I wanted the chess pieces. I couldn't recall ever playing. That was the thing—Kader didn't play.

The military symbols were present because I'd been told I'd been trained, a killer ready to take commands.

That was why they'd saved and rebuilt me.

The skills were still there but the dedication was not. It was meticulously whittled away, piece by piece, with each surgery and each debriefing. Both procedures were daunting and degrading. I wasn't a person but a machine who owed his country his life.

After more time than I care to admit, it became crystal clear that no one cared about me or the man I'd been. They told me that they'd invested in me and that was why they wouldn't allow me to die in the explosion.

They'd lied.

Because that man, Mason Pierce, was dead.

They hadn't only allowed it—they'd facilitated it.

My commitment and dedication were no longer given freely to anyone but myself.

Leaning forward, I stared into my own eyes.

"Why the fuck are you so obsessed with Laurel Carlson?"

My reflection didn't respond, not verbally.

Instead, I scanned my cheekbones, my nose, my lips, and my chin.

Slipping on a long-sleeved t-shirt and lightweight sleeping pants, I covered my colors, my hidden pictures and forgotten memories. Laurel might have asked to see them, but she didn't understand.

Step by step, I made my way to the bedroom door and flipped on the light.

Fuck, I should turn around. I shouldn't be here, not now.

My adrenaline was still too high after disposing of Cartwright's body.

My fingers balled into tight fists as I took her in.

She was still asleep, curled on her side.

My feet weren't listening to my brain. They weren't the only part of my body.

With each step closer to the bed, the harder my dick became. Listening to her soft breaths and watching her tits rise and fall were aphrodisiacs to my blood. Self-control was out of reach as my circulation rushed to one destination.

Turning off the light, I closed the door.

My dick ached with need as my balls grew tighter.

.s a fucking voyeur in this room, even in the dark.

all that had happened, I claimed it. My hand snaked

ɔw the band of my pants and gripped the width of my

.ɪck.

Not only had those doctors saved my face and hands, they'd managed to leave my dick fully functional. Right now, it wanted to wake her from her slumber and function.

Was it to get her out of my system and finish this assignment, punish her for fucking with my thoughts and life, or was it for more —to keep her?

LAUREL

Something jarred me awake. I wasn't sure how long I'd slept. The colors were now gone as were my yoga pants and Kader's sweatshirt. The room was saturated in darkness. I couldn't see my clothing, but by the feel of the sheets beneath me, a shirt and panties seemed to be the answer to what I was currently wearing. Yet none of that mattered.

He'd kept his promise. I knew that I wasn't alone.

"Kader?"

"It's done."

The deep voice echoed through the cool air as the image of Russ returned to my memory. Tears prickled behind my eyes and I reached out into the darkness. "Where are you?"

"I'm here as I said I would be."

He was in the room but his voice was coming from the far wall.

I shifted to sitting. "What...how did you...?"

"I did what I needed to do, for you."

"Where is he?"

"You don't want to know, and even if you do, I'm not telling you."

I fumbled around the bed, patting the surface.

"I have the remote."

"Turn on the light."

"Not yet."

There was something in the timbre of his response.

"Kader?"

"Laurel."

Though I had said his name as a question, the way he said mine brought heat to my core. The thought of what could happen next twisted my insides. My mind knew it was wrong to want Kader, especially now.

I should be thinking about Russ and our research.

I was tired of thinking about that. At the moment, I craved contact, something to remind me that I was still alive. Call it Stockholm syndrome or maybe it was Prince Charming.

Kader saved me, the damsel in distress.

Prior to this awful, twisted chain of events, that was never a description I would have given myself. Now it seemed fitting.

"If you're thinking about..." I began as the heat within my

circulation grew hotter by the millisecond, sending lightning bolts between my legs. I squeezed my thighs together as the memory of his tongue came back with a vengeance. "I-I meant what I said the other day and I still mean it. I want you. And right now, I need you."

"Fuck, Laurel, you don't know what you're saying."

"Maybe I don't." I threw back the covers and placing my bare feet on the cool concrete, I stood. "If you don't want me like that, let me give you something, something for what you did...all you've done." I knelt on the floor and placed my hands behind my back as butterflies took wing in my stomach. "I won't touch you, just my mouth."

Something resembling a growl resonated through the room.

"Stand the fuck up." His grip came to my arm, painfully jerking me back to my feet.

"Hey."

"You're not a whore. Don't act like one."

"I'm not. I'm..."

His hold of my arm tightened as his face came closer in the darkness. "Tell me, what is your charge: a blow job for me going down on you or maybe for cleaning up your dead lover?"

"Stop it. That wasn't what I meant..." Like a bucket of cold water, the realization drenched me with the knowledge that he'd turned me down again. It was obvious my feelings weren't reciprocated. I pulled my arm free. "Then get out. I'm tired of being turned down. You don't want me. Fine. I'll never bring it up again." When he didn't answer, I raised my volume. "Get out. Just leave me alone."

The tears were back, filling my eyes and threatening to fall to my cheeks.

I hated what they implied.

I'd never been the kind of woman to cry. This reaction was more than Kader's rejection. It was Russ and the loss of our figurative baby, our life's work.

"Is that what you think?" His voice was still close, so close that the warmth of his breath skirted across my skin. The fresh scent that I'd noticed after his shower was back, surrounding us. Yet before I could give it much thought or was able to get back into the bed, an arm wrapped around my midsection pulling me backward.

I gasped, instinctively reaching for his arm and gripping the material of his sleeve as his erection pushed, hard and angry, against my lower back.

"Do you think I don't want you, that I don't want to fuck you right now?"

"You said—"

In one swift motion, he'd moved me, moved us.

The coolness of a concrete wall was in front of me while the fire within him burned behind me.

Kader lifted my hands to the cement blocks after whisking the t-shirt over my head. The cool air prickled my heated skin. His lips came to my neck with nips as his fingers tweaked my breasts. His touch was a flame and his deep voice a blowtorch. "I fucking want you. I want all of you because I can't get you out of my head. You're fucking with my decisions and my willpower." With each statement his hands roamed, leaving my flesh in ashes, consumed by his fire. "I can't fight it any longer—I won't. I am going to bury my dick where my tongue has been."

"Yes," I moaned.

"Don't let go."

It was the same thing he'd said about the headboard. This time, I splayed my fingers over the rough concrete blocks as my panties disappeared into the darkness. A nudge with his foot to the inside of my ankles and my legs spread. His fingers came to rest on my hips as he pulled my backside toward him, close enough that his hard rod nudged my lower back.

"I'm going to take you and erase every other fucking man from your memory."

"Please, I want to see you," I panted as two long fingers found their way to my core. "Oh."

"No. You don't need to see, Laurel. You're going to feel me. You're going to know I'm there. And when I'm done, your pussy will remember how it felt."

His declarations echoed through the room as his ministrations continued to send shock waves to my toes.

"Ride my fingers. I need you ready to take what I have to give you."

My knees bent and straightened as I shamelessly did as he'd instructed. The wanton need mushroomed within me growing with each bounce, flowing like electricity, and rushing through my bloodstream.

"I-I can't..."

His actions were all-encompassing. They weren't concentrated on my pussy, though that was where they originated. Similar to throwing a rock into a stream, the resulting waves rippled endlessly to both shores.

That was what was happening.

With only his touch, he dominated everything within me.

Kader was the choreographer and I was his dancer. My feet stretched until I was lifted to the tips of my toes before he'd release me back to a plié. When I thought the dance was near its climax, a spin of my body and a pirouette.

"Fuck." His curse preceded his next move. Before I knew it, we were back where we'd been the other day, my hands on the metal headboard and Kader over me. The only difference was that this time, I was on my knees with my backside in the air.

His grasp of my hips intensified as the head of his cock moved up and down my folds.

"Please."

There was no way I could have prepared for the consequence of my plea. My whimper echoed off the concrete walls as my body clamped down, resisting the invasion.

What the hell was inside me?

There was no way he was that big.

Kader's body stilled as tears broke free, spilling over my lids.

"Talk to me."

"You're...is that you?"

A deep laugh filled my ears as the body above me vibrated accordingly.

Was he really laughing?

He rarely smiled and now he was laughing.

His reaction brought a smile to my face as I willed myself to relax. With each passing second his presence became less painful and more manageable. "I'm...okay. Don't stop. I want this. You were right. I feel you." No longer still, he began to ease in and out as the pleasure built.

The friction increased as my essence created a soothing medium.

The pressure on my hips didn't match his speed.

I lowered my forehead to the pillow as we moved within the rhythm he'd created.

"Please," I said. "I want *you*. Don't hold back."

Again he stilled. "You don't know what you're asking."

Pulling away, I flipped to my back, baring myself in the darkness. My arms surrounded his neck as my fingers entwined in his damp hair. It was my confirmation that he'd showered. Instead of wrenching away from my touch, he allowed me to bring him closer.

"I want *you*," I repeated.

His lips crashed with mine as in one thrust he filled me completely. My back arched and a moan broke through our kiss as our new position allowed him to go deeper than before.

"Are you sure?"

Before answering, I moved my grasp from his neck to his shoulders, gripping the soft material. "I'm holding on."

There was a noise like a scoff as he did as I asked.

The other morning he'd marked me.

This went beyond that.

It was more, so much more.

A connection that felt unique.

A scoff and earlier a laugh.

His tempo varied as I teetered between unimaginable pleasure and occasional pain. Both were delivered by not only his giant cock, but his hands and mouth. When we were done, there would be no part of me left unmarked.

As the muscles in his shoulders began to strain, his pace slowed and he reached between us, finding my tender, swollen clit. Like a strike to flint, his touch was fire to a short fuse.

Unable to refrain, I screamed out.

My entire body convulsed as I held on to his thick neck.

As the echoes of my ecstasy began to fade, beneath my touch his muscles grew taut. No longer still, the concrete room filled with the same sound that had woken me the other day.

It had been a roar.

It hadn't been a lion.

The beast had a name.

Kader.

I wrapped my arms tighter around his neck as I buried my face in his shoulder.

This wasn't the time to cry, but that didn't stop my reaction.

"I didn't mean to hurt you," he said after a kiss to my forehead.

"It's not that."

Pushing up with his arms, he eased out of me. "I shouldn't—"

I lifted my finger to his lips. "It was..." I feigned a smile though he couldn't see me. "God, it was...mostly great."

"Mostly?"

Was there humor in his tone?

"I think I need practice."

The bed started to shift and I reached for his hand. "Don't leave. Please stay here."

With a sigh, he lifted the covers over me.

I waited for the door, for the indication he'd walked away. Instead, after a moment, the blankets moved. "You need to scoot over if you want me to stay."

"You'll stay?"

"I'm tired. The *door to the outside is locked.*"

Was that a yes?

Excitement sparked to life as I slid over toward the wall. The mattress moved as he lay down and pulled the covers over both of us.

Within the eye of the storm, I'd found a stranger to protect me from dangers I didn't understand. As we settled in beside one another, I relished his warmth. When I turned on my side facing him, I realized that not only was he wearing a t-shirt, but his legs were covered in soft pants.

"I think this dress code is unfair," I said.

Kader rolled toward me as his large palm skirted over my skin; from my shoulder it went down over my breast, waist, and hip. It came to a stop as his fingers splayed over the soft flesh of my backside. "I don't know. It seems fair to me."

"I don't know how I became your job. I really know nothing about you or who hired you, but thank you for doing your job and keeping me safe."

For longer than I expected, silence settled over the room. It was as his hand on my backside flexed, pulling me closer to his warmth that he replied, "You're mistaken. That wasn't what I was hired to do."

"It wasn't?"

"No. I was hired to kill you."

Kader and Laurel's story continues in *OBSESSED* and concludes in *BOUND*. You're not going to want to miss a moment of *TANGLED WEB*.

If you're enjoying *TANGLED WEB*, don't miss *WEB OF SIN*, the trilogy is complete. Turn to the next page for a peek at *SECRETS*, book #1, *WEB OF SIN*.

A PEEK AT SECRETS, BOOK #1 WEB OF SIN

Araneae

PROLOGUE

*M*y mother's fingers blanched as she gripped the steering wheel tighter with each turn. The traffic on the interstate seemed to barely move, yet we continued to swerve in, out, and around other cars. From my angle I couldn't read the speedometer, though I knew we were bordering on reckless driving. I jumped, holding my breath as we pulled in front of the monstrous semi, the blare of a truck's horn filling our ears. Tons of metal and sixteen wheels screeched as brakes locked behind us, yet my mother's erratic driving continued.

"Listen very carefully," she said, her words muffled by the quagmire of whatever she was about to say, the weight pulling

them down as she fluttered her gaze between the road ahead
and the rearview mirror.

"Mom, you're scaring me."

I reached for the handle of the car door and held on as if
the seat belt couldn't keep me safe while she continued to
weave from lane to lane.

"Your father," she began, "made mistakes, deadly
mistakes."

My head shook side to side. "No, Dad was a good man.
Why would you say that?"

My father, the man I called Dad for as long as I could
remember, was the epitome of everything good: honest and
hardworking, a faithful husband, and an omnipresent father.

He *was*.

He died less than a week ago.

"Listen, child. Don't interrupt me." She reached into her
purse with one hand while the other gripped tighter to the
wheel. Removing an envelope from the depths of the bag, she
handed it my direction. "Take this. Inside are your plane tick-
ets. God knows if I could afford to send you away farther than
Colorado, I would."

My fingers began to tremble as I looked down at the envelope in my grasp. "You're sending me away?" The words were
barely audible as my throat tightened and heaviness weighed
down upon my chest. "Mom—"

Her chin lifted in the way it did when her mind was set. I
had a million visions of the times I'd seen her stand up for
what she believed. At only five feet three, she was a pit bull in

a toy poodle body. That didn't mean her bark was worse than her bite. No, my mother always followed through. In all things she was a great example of survival and fortitude.

"When I say your father," she went on, "I don't mean my husband—may the Lord rest his soul. Byron was a good man who gave his...everything...for you, for *us*. He and I have always been honest with you. We wanted you to know that we loved you as our own. God knows that I wanted to give birth. I tried to get pregnant for years. When you were presented to us, we knew you were a gift from heaven." Her bloodshot eyes —those from crying through the past week since the death of my dad—briefly turned my direction and then back to the highway. "Renee, never doubt that you're our angel. However, the reality is somewhere darker. The devil has been searching for you. And my greatest fear has always been that he'd find you."

The devil?

My skin peppered with goose bumps as I imagined the biblical creature: male-like with red skin, pointed teeth, and a pitchfork. Surely that wasn't what she meant?

Her next words brought me back to reality.

"I used to wake in a cold sweat, fearing the day had arrived. It's no longer a nightmare. You've been found."

"Found? I don't understand."

"Your biological father made a deal against the devil. He thought if he did what was right, he could... well, he could *survive*. The woman who gave birth to you was my best friend —a long time ago. We hadn't been in contact for years. She hoped that would secure your safety and keep you hidden. That deal...it didn't work the way he hoped. Saving themselves was a long shot. Their hope was to save you. That's how you became our child."

It was more information than I'd ever been told. I have always known I was adopted but nothing more. There was a promise of *one day*. I used to hope for that time to come. With the lead weight in the pit of my stomach, I knew that now that *one day* had arrived, and I wasn't ready. I wanted more time.

The only woman I knew as my mother shook her head just before wiping a tear from her cheek. "I prayed you'd be older before we had this talk, that you would be able to comprehend the gravity of this information. But as I said, things have changed."

The writing on the envelope blurred as tears filled my sixteen-year-old eyes. The man I knew as my dad was gone, and now the woman who had raised me was sending me away. "Where are you sending me?"

"Colorado. There's a boarding school in the mountains, St. Mary of the Forest. It's private and elite. They'll protect you."

I couldn't comprehend. "For how long? What about you? What about my friends? When will I be able to come home?"

"You'll stay until you're eighteen and graduated. And then it will be up to you. There's no coming back here...ever. This city isn't home, not anymore. I'm leaving Chicago, too, as soon as I get you out." Her neck stiffened as she swallowed her tears. "We both have to be brave. I thought at first

Byron's accident was just that—an accident. But then this morning...I knew. Our time is up. They'll kill me if they find me, just as they did Byron. And Renee..." She looked my way, her gray eyes swirling with emotion. While I'd expect sadness, it was fear that dominated. "...my fate would be easy compared to yours."

She cleared her throat, pretending that tears weren't cascading down her pale cheeks.

"Honey, these people are dangerous. They don't mess around, and they don't play fair. We don't know how, but they found you, and your dad paid the price. I will forever believe that he died to protect you. That's why we have this small window of time. I want you to know that if necessary, I'll do the same. The thing is, my death won't stop them. And no matter what, I won't hand you over."

"Hand me over?"

We swerved again, barreling down an exit until Mom slammed on her brakes, leaving us in bumper-to-bumper traffic. Her gaze again went to the rearview mirror.

"Are we being followed?" I asked.

Instead of answering, she continued her instructions. "In that envelope is information for your new identity, a trust fund, and where you'll be living. Your dad and I had this backup plan waiting. We hoped we'd never have to use it, but he insisted on being prepared." Her gaze went upward. "Thank you, Byron. You're still watching over us from heaven."

Slowly, I peeled back the envelope's flap and pulled out

two Colorado driver's licenses. They both contained my picture—that was the only recognizable part. The name, address, and even birth dates were different. "Kennedy Hawkins," I said, the fictitious name thick on my tongue.

"Why are there two?"

"Look at the dates. Use the one that makes you eighteen years old for this flight. It's to ensure the airline will allow you to fly unaccompanied. Once you're in Colorado, destroy the one with the added two years. The school needs your real age for your grade in school."

I stared down at one and then the other. The name was the same. I repeated it again, "Kennedy Hawkins."

"Learn it. Live it. Become Kennedy."

A never-before-thought-of question came to my mind. "Did I have a different name before I came to you?"

My mother's eyes widened as her pallid complexion changed from white to gray. "It's better if you don't know."

I sat taller in the seat, mimicking the strength she'd shown me all of my life. "You're sending me away. You're saying we may never see one another again. This is my only chance. I think I deserve to be told everything."

"Not everything." She blinked rapidly. "About your name, your dad and I decided to alter your birth name, not change it completely. You were very young, and we hoped having a derivation of what you'd heard would help make the transition easier. Of course, we gave you our last name."

"My real name isn't Renee? What is it?"

"Araneae."

The syllables played on repeat in my head, bringing back memories I couldn't catch. "I've heard that before, but not as a name."

She nodded. "I always thought it was ironic how you loved insects. Your name means spider. Your birth mother thought it gave you strength, a hard outer shell, and the ability to spin silk, beautiful and strong."

"Araneae," I repeated aloud.

Her stern stare turned my way. "Forget that name. Forget Araneae and Renee. We were wrong to allow you any connection. Embrace Kennedy."

My heart beat rapidly in my chest as I examined all of the paperwork. My parents, the ones I knew, were thorough in their plan B. I had a birth certificate, a Social Security card, a passport matching the more accurate age, and the driver's license that I'd seen earlier, all with my most recent school picture. According to the documentation, my parents' names were Phillip and Debbie Hawkins. The perfect boring family. Boring or exciting, family was something I would never have again.

"And what happened to Phillip and Debbie?" I asked as if any of this made sense.

"They died in an automobile accident. Their life insurance funded your trust fund. You are an only child."

The car crept forward in the line of traffic near the departure terminal of O'Hare Airport. A million questions swirled through my head, and yet I struggled to voice even one. I reached out to my mother's arm. "I don't want to leave you."

"I'll always be with you, always."

"How will we talk?"

She lifted her fist to her chest. "In here. Listen to your heart."

Pulling to the curb and placing the car in park, she leaned my direction and wrapped me in her arms. The familiar scent of lotions and perfumes comforted me as much as her hug. "Know you're loved. Never forget that, Kennedy."

I swallowed back the tears brought on by her calling me by the unfamiliar name.

She reached for her wrist and unclasped the bracelet she always wore. "I want you to have this."

I shook my head. "Mom, I never remember seeing you without it."

"It's very important. I've protected it as I have you. Now, I'm giving it to you." She forced a smile. "Maybe it will remind you of me."

"Mom, I'd never forget you." I looked down to the gold bracelet in the palm of my hand as my mom picked it up, the small charms dangling as she secured it around my wrist.

"Now, it's time for you to go."

"I don't know what to do."

"You do. Go to the counter for the airlines. Hand them your ticket and the correct identification. Stay strong."

"What about those people?" I asked. "Who are they? Will you be safe?"

"I'll worry about me once I'm sure that you're safe."

"I don't even know who they are."

Her gaze moved from me to the world beyond the windshield. For what seemed like hours, she stared as the slight glint of sunshine reflected on the frost-covered January ground. Snow spit through the air, blowing in waves. Finally, she spoke, "Never repeat the name."

"What name?"

"Swear it," she said, her voice trembling with emotion.

It was almost too much. I nodded.

"No. I need to hear you promise me. This name can never be spoken aloud."

"I swear," I said.

"Sparrow, Allister Sparrow. He's currently in charge, but one day it will be his son, Sterling."

I wished for a pen to write the names down; however, from the way they sent a chill down my spine, I was most certain that I'd never forget.

WEB OF SIN is completely available: *SECRETS*, *LIES*, and *PROMISES*.

WHAT TO DO NOW

LEND IT: Did you enjoy TWISTED? Do you have a friend who'd enjoy TWISTED? TWISTED may be lent one time. Sharing is caring!

RECOMMEND IT: Do you have multiple friends who'd enjoy my dark romance with twists and turns and an all new sexy and infuriating anti-hero? Tell them about it! Call, text, post, tweet...your recommendation is the nicest gift you can give to an author!

REVIEW IT: Tell the world. Please go to the retailer where you purchased this book, as well as Goodreads, and write a review. Please share your thoughts about TWISTED on:

*Amazon, TWISTED Customer Reviews

*Barnes & Noble, TWISTED, Customer Reviews

*iBooks, TWISTED Customer Reviews

* BookBub, TWISTED Customer Reviews

*Goodreads.com/Aleatha Romig

MORE FROM ALEATHA:

If you enjoyed SECRETS and want more from Aleatha, check out her backlist encompassing many of your favorite genres.

WEB OF SIN TRILOGY (Dark romance trilogy)
SECRETS
LIES
PROMISES

THE CONSEQUENCES SERIES: (bestselling dark romance)
(First in the series FREE)
CONSEQUENCES
TRUTH
CONVICTED
REVEALED

BEYOND THE CONSEQUENCES
BEHIND HIS EYES CONSEQUENCES
BEHIND HIS EYES TRUTH
RIPPLES (A Consequences stand-alone novel)

STAND ALONE MAFIA THRILLER:

PRICE OF HONOR
Available Now

THE INFIDELITY SERIES: (acclaimed romantic saga)
(First in the series FREE)
BETRAYAL
CUNNING
DECEPTION
ENTRAPMENT
FIDELITY

INSIDIOUS (stand-alone smart, sexy thriller):

THE LIGHT DUET: (romantic thriller duet)
INTO THE LIGHT
AWAY FROM THE DARK

THE UN-NOVELLAS: (short, erotic reads exploring
hidden fantasies)
UNCONVENTIONAL
UNEXPECTED

ALEATHA'S LIGHTER ONES (stand-alone light, fun, and sexy romances guaranteed to leave you with a smile and maybe a tear)

PLUS ONE

A SECRET ONE

ANOTHER ONE (free novella)

ONE NIGHT

ABOUT THE AUTHOR

Aleatha Romig is a New York Times, Wall Street Journal, and USA Today bestselling author who lives in Indiana, USA. She has raised three children with her high school sweetheart and husband of over thirty years. Before she became a full-time author, she worked days as a dental hygienist and spent her nights writing. Now, when she's not imagining mind-blowing twists and turns, she likes to spend her time with her family and friends. Her other pastimes include reading and creating heroes/anti-heroes who haunt your dreams!

Aleatha impresses with her versatility in writing. She released her first novel, CONSEQUENCES, in August of 2011. CONSEQUENCES, a dark romance, became a bestselling series with five novels and two companions released from 2011 through 2015. The compelling and epic story of Anthony and Claire Rawlings has graced more than half a million e-readers. Her first stand-alone smart, sexy thriller INSIDIOUS was next. Then Aleatha released the five-novel INFIDELITY series, a romantic suspense saga, that took the reading world by storm, the final book landing on three of the top bestseller lists. She ventured into traditional publishing with Thomas and Mercer. Her books INTO THE LIGHT and AWAY FROM THE DARK were published through this mystery/thriller publisher in 2016. In the spring of 2017, Aleatha again ventured into a different genre with her first fun and sexy stand-alone romantic comedy with the USA Today bestseller PLUS ONE. She continued with ONE NIGHT and ANOTHER ONE. If you like fun, sexy, novellas that make your heart pound, try her UNCONVENTIONAL and UNEXPECTED. In 2018 Aleatha returned to her dark romance roots with WEB OF SIN.

Aleatha is a "Published Author's Network" member of the Romance Writers of America and PEN America. She is represented by Kevan Lyon of Marsal Lyon Literary Agency.

facebook.com/aleatharomig

twitter.com/aleatharomig

instagram.com/aleatharomig

CPSIA information can be obtained
at www.ICGtesting.com
Printed in the USA
LVHW031558060619
620404LV00036B/648